D1572012

Waiting in the Shadows

Waiting in the Shadows

The Stewarts of Stormhaven - 3

Marilyn Ross

Five Star • Waterville, Maine

Published in 2004 in conjunction with
Maureen Moran Agency.

The text of this edition is unabridged.

Set in 11 pt. Plantin by Al Chase.

Printed in the United States on permanent paper.

Library of Congress Cataloging-in-Publication Data

Ross, Marilyn, 1912–
    Waiting in the shadows / Marilyn Ross.
       p. cm.—(The Stewarts of Stormhaven ; 3)
    ISBN 1-59414-244-0 (hc : alk. paper)
    1. Remarried people—Fiction. 2. Married women—
Fiction. 3. Scotland—Fiction. I. Title.
PR9199.3.R5996W35 2004
813′.54—dc22
                                  2004053228

To my good neighbors,
Gladys and Campbell Mackay

Prologue

The Stewarts of Stormhaven!

It is the year 1831. Thirty years have passed since young Dr. Ian Stewart and his lovely wife Ann began their married life in the ancient house in Edinburgh next to Mercy Cemetery. It was there in that old house, whose cellars became known as the "Cellars Of The Dead," that the dedicated fledgling doctor and his wife met with threats to their lives and a series of macabre events that nearly drove them away from the ancient city.

The present story deals with the daughter of Dr. Ian Stewart and his wife. It tells of her going to London and finding a rich young husband, and of the horror that she found there, waiting in the shadows.

Ishbel was the only child of Dr. Ian Stewart and Ann, so it was to be expected that they would attempt to give her every benefit. She resembled her attractive, auburn-haired mother to a remarkable degree but had the serious gray eyes of her father.

Stormhaven Castle still stood in majesty overlooking the City of Edinburgh. Both the elder Ian Stewart, who had so long headed the family banking firm, and his wife Flora, the doctor's daughter from Glasgow, were dead. Ian Stewart the elder had died of a stroke in 1815, and in 1820 Flora had succumbed to pneumonia.

Walter Stewart had taken his father's place as head of the bank and was grooming his nephew Ernest to succeed him. Ernest was the twenty-one-year-old son of Roger Stewart, who had become one of Scotland's most important shipbuilders.

Dr. Ian Stewart and Ann had moved to a new and larger house near Stormhaven. Ian still had a busy medical practice, but his activity had been curtailed by severe bronchial attacks that often laid him low for days at a time. Ann, who was in excellent health, was his faithful and patient nurse during these distressing periods. She knew that her husband had been upset by their only child's going to London to live. And the scant number of letters Ishbel wrote them failed to keep them well informed of her life there.

Henry Davis, Ishbel's wealthy, tea-merchant husband, had seemed a nice enough person. On the other hand, they had not known him long enough, they felt, to form an accurate opinion of him. They knew he'd been married before and had been left a widower by the death of his wife in a tragic accident, but he'd told them little else.

There were few of the old generation left who remembered the bad days at Stormhaven when the ghost of the highwayman, Black Charlie, had stalked the grounds and house. One of them was Dr. Jock Gregory, retired from the medical school of Edinburgh University and living with Dr. Ian and Ann now. The old man was eighty-four years old, but except for being thinner, he had not changed much. His mind was as lively as in his earlier years and he often gave guest lectures at the university.

Dr. Jock Gregory had been a rival of the elder Ian Stewart for Flora's hand. And when he'd failed to win her, he'd continued to be a friend of the two. Now he was a friend of their son and, as it was to turn out, of their granddaughter Ishbel. But this was still ahead—part of a series of terrifying events that would take place in London!

Chapter One

Ishbel Stewart Davis came to a halt about midway along the gravel path that bisected the garden and glanced up at the full, pale moon. The silver of its beams flooded the garden, giving it an eerie beauty. In the background rose the dark, squarish shadow of the old mansion at Number Twenty-Two Castle Square. Even though this June night in 1831 was pleasantly warm for London, Ishbel gave a tiny shudder.

Her thoughts rather than the night could be blamed for her involuntary shiver. A while earlier she had heard her husband Henry enter the house and go directly to his study. He had been absent since he'd left for his office in the morning, which was common enough these days. She had wanted to see him and talk with him, so she had waited for a short spell and then had gone down and knocked on the door of the study.

There had been no answer! She had stood there with dismay shadowing her lovely, delicate face. After a few seconds she had knocked again, and still there was no answer. Yet she knew he had to be in there. As she stood in the shadowed hallway waiting, a figure glided into view and paused when Ishbel's presence was noticed.

Standing a distance from her in his black silken suit and round, black cap was Chen, her husband's personal servant. The old Chinese, whom Henry's father had brought back from one of his many trips to the Orient, was devoted to Henry. Ishbel had always felt that the bland-faced old Chinese with his long pigtail and quiet mien resented her.

Holding her head high in a casual assurance she did not

feel, the auburn-haired Ishbel asked Chen, "Have you seen my husband?"

Chen stood humbly with hands clasped before him. He shook his head. "No, missee."

She did not believe him. She said, "I'm certain I heard him come in. He must be in his study. The door is locked, but he doesn't answer."

"Perhaps he locked it before he left this morning, missee," the inscrutable old Chinese replied.

Ishbel knew he was being evasive. It was nothing new. Chen always took her husband's side and protected him as much as he could. She said resentfully, "I know he has to be in there."

Chen shrugged. "I did not hear him, missee." And he turned to vanish in the shadows as quickly as he had appeared.

She watched after him, thinking bitterly that he was the epitome of everything about the old mansion. Shrouded in mystery, the ancient Chen nearly always suggested hostility towards her, a hostility carefully hidden but which existed nevertheless. Ishbel knew that in his tiny cubicle of a bedroom Chen had some sort of idol of Buddha, before which he lighted offerings of incense and chanted strange prayers in his native language. Prayers against herself, she found herself suspecting.

She turned and raised her fist to knock on the study door once more but changed her mind. Instead, she placed her ear close to the door, and from inside there seemed to come the thin murmur of angry voices. Her husband's voice and that of someone else! But whose? She listened hard but couldn't make enough of the snatches of voices that came in blurred fashion through the heavy oaken door.

It was not the first time something like this had taken place. There had been other nights when she'd been sure she'd heard strange voices downstairs in the late hours. Henry had always denied it, but she'd believed he was lying. After listening at the door for a moment, she decided to leave for a little and take a stroll in the garden at the rear of the mansion.

Stepping into the fresh, aromatic air of the garden, she at once felt a little less nervous. She walked hesitantly along the gravel path that led to the red brick wall at the rear of the garden. It was a place of refuge, somewhere to be alone and grapple with her frightened thoughts. What sort of game was Henry playing with her? How had their happy married life come to this sad pass?

Her mind moved quickly back in time to the afternoon of that garden party at the Duchess of Clarewill's, where she had gone as a guest of her closest girl friend, Jane Gray. Ishbel had come to London as a guest of the Grays. The garden party given by the Duchess was said to be the number one social occasion of the London summer season. It was 1824, and Ishbel was making her first visit to the great English city.

The colorful gardens, with their tall, sparkling fountains, had fascinated her. The women, in white dresses and carrying parasols, and the men, in light gray frock coats and gray top hats, had seemed much more fashionable than their counterparts in Edinburgh.

Jane had left Ishbel for a moment to go and chat a little with some other friends she'd spotted in the distance, and Ishbel had found herself standing alone as a good-looking, dark-haired man came over to her and, removing his hat, bowed and presented himself.

With a faint smile, he said, "I have just talked with Jane. She suggested that I come over and keep you company. My name is Henry Davis and I know Jane well. And you are the girl from Scotland."

She smiled in return. "I am Ishbel Stewart and my home is in Edinburgh."

"Are you enjoying London?"

"Very much."

"I like your Scottish accent," he said. "It is a refreshing change to hear that slight burr."

Ishbel blushed. "I have not cultivated it. It's the way we speak in Edinburgh."

Henry Davis said, "I know. I have visited your city. You are one of the banking Stewarts?"

"Yes. My father's cousin, Walter Stewart, is now head of the bank, a post held by my late grandfather until his death. My father is a doctor."

The young man looked interested. "I had an idea all the family were in banking."

"No. I have an uncle who is a shipbuilder."

"And what about you?" he asked. "What are your plans for the future?"

"I have nothing definite in mind. My father would like to see me continue my education. I have an interest in art and may decide to take additional lessons in painting."

"Excellent! I have an aunt, Betsy Davis by name, who paints very well on chinaware."

"That can be difficult. She must have talent."

The young man laughed good-naturedly. "She's an eccentric old girl! Very fond of cats—must have a dozen of them. But she does have a gift for art."

Ishbel glanced around her at the groups of well-dressed men and women in the huge, colorful gardens. "This is an exciting affair!"

"You think so?"

"I do. Don't you?"

"Not really. I came because I like the Duke and Duchess.

Frankly, each year it begins to be a bit more of a bore!"

Ishbel said, "You forget I am new to it all."

"Edinburgh has its own social life."

"But nothing on the scale of this. Of course England, and especially London, has so much to offer! So many wonders!"

His pleasant gray eyes sought hers. "May I have the privilege of showing some of them to you? Do you plan to be here long?"

"A month anyway."

Henry Davis said, "Then let me be your guide part of the time."

"That is very kind of you."

"Not at all. I am a tea importer. While I'm very busy when ships come in, I have long intervals when the office runs very well without me."

"How lucky you are."

He smiled again. "Only when I have someone to share those idle hours with me."

That was the start! From the very beginning she liked Henry Davis tremendously. When she returned home with Jane and they were together in the privacy of Jane's bedroom, she'd asked the pretty, blonde English girl, "What about Henry Davis?"

There was a mischievous twinkle in Jane's large blue eyes as she and Ishbel sat on the edge of Jane's bed. Jane said, "I knew you'd like him!"

"He seems very nice," she admitted. "But then I know nothing much about him. Except that he wants to call on me and show me around London."

Jane clapped her hands with delight. "That's even better than I hoped for!"

"It is?"

"Yes. I had an idea you two would get along well. But you

13

have surpassed my hopes."

Ishbel blushed. "I have made him no promise. First, tell me about him."

Her friend said, "He'll do things the right way—call on father and mother first and then ask us both out, if I'm not mistaken. He and my fiancé, Captain Eric Grant of the Guards, are good friends. Henry will probably try to arrange for a double date."

Ishbel raised a hand to halt the other girl's speculations. Plaintively, she begged her, "Will you first tell me just a little about him?"

"He's a widower."

"A widower? He seems very young for that."

"He is. It was a tragic business. His wife Patricia was the daughter of Lord Carney. Henry married into the nobility."

"What happened to this Patricia?"

"She died in a fall at Number Twenty-Two, Castle Square."

"Castle Square?"

"Yes. That is where the Davis mansion is. It's a most fashionable section of Mayfair."

Ishbel frowned slightly. "You say his wife died from a fall that took place in their home?"

Jane nodded. "Yes."

"Wasn't that unusual?"

"It was a shocking thing! From all accounts she was on her way down the rear stairway, which is very long and steep. She apparently caught her heel in the carpeting and fell the full length of the steps. Henry heard her scream as she fell. He was in his study at the time and rushed out to help her. But it was too late. She had broken her neck in the fall."

"How dreadful for him!"

"He has only lately returned to society," Jane declared,

14

"and he has shown little interest in anything or anyone. But now it appears that you have caught his fancy."

"Not really," Ishbel protested. "He explained to me that his tea importing business gives him a lot of free time. He offered to spend some of it showing me London."

"It's a splendid offer. If he calls, you must take him up on it. It would be good for you and excellent for him."

"He'll likely forget all about it," Ishbel said.

"I doubt that," Jane replied. "He's not that sort."

Jane's prediction proved correct. The following day Henry Davis paid a call at the Gray home. And after he had a short conversation with Mrs. Gray, the girls joined him and he broached a plan to take them to the theater in the company of Captain Eric Grant.

Smiling at Ishbel, he said, "I'm sure you'd enjoy the new comedy at the Haymarket. You must not leave London without seeing some theater."

Of course the girls agreed. A few evenings later Henry Davis arrived, accompanied by Captain Eric Grant. The young Guards officer proved to be a pleasant-faced fop with a tendency to laugh at odd times. It took Ishbel only a short while to realize the young man was not too bright and his laugh was a nervous habit. Jane didn't seem to mind this; when in the company of the tall young man, she kept regarding him with adoring eyes.

The play at the Haymarket proved pleasant. Henry Davis showed himself adept at getting them a hansom cab in the crowded street after the show. He gave the driver the address of a restaurant not far away in the West End and got in the cab to sit beside Ishbel.

"I have ordered a light supper for us," he said. "I hope you do not object."

"Not unless Jane does," she said, glancing across to the

opposite seat in the dark interior of the cab, where the Captain and Jane were holding hands.

"I'm frantically hungry!" Jane exclaimed. "I look forward to supper!"

Henry smiled at Ishbel. "I assume that settles the matter."

The cab rattled over the cobblestone streets and finally came to a halt at a gaslit corner. There they descended from the cab and Henry paid the driver his fare. Then they walked to the entrance of an establishment with glowing, multipaned windows, curtained so that one could not see inside. Above its door hung a sign in old English, gray lettering on a white background, which announced it to be Hancock's Tavern.

"I think you will like it," Henry promised Ishbel as they led the way in.

As they entered the narrow entrance corridor, another fashionable party made their way out. Three men and a woman of young middle age paused to let them enter. Ishbel gave them only a passing glance, but she saw that one bore heavy pock marks on his face, one was stout and the other male had a lean, rather weary look. The woman was plain of face and of dress.

As they passed, Henry politely thanked the party for waiting for them to enter. Inside the tavern a stout man in a dark frock coat and trousers greeted them. He shook hands with Henry warmly and informed him, "I have reserved a table for you at the rear: in an ell where you may have privacy, sir."

"Thank you," Henry said. And they all followed the stout man through the maze of busy tables to a section of the big room that jogged to the left. There an empty table in a quiet spot awaited them.

When they were all seated and the stout man had gone to

order their food, Jane leaned across the table and asked Ishbel, "Did you recognize anyone in that group who waited for us to pass them in the entry?"

"No," she said. "Should I have?"

"Not really," her friend replied. "But the tallest one was Thomas De Quincey, the famous writer."

Ishbel at once recognized the name. "You mean the one who wrote *Confessions Of An Opium Eater*?"

"Yes," Jane said. "I would have expected you to recognize him, Henry."

Henry's handsome face shadowed with annoyance. "Why on earth? I'm interested neither in him nor his opium eating!"

Jane protested, "But he is a fine writer! Everyone reads his essays in *Blackwood's Magazine*."

Captain Eric Grant gave one of his nervous laughs and at the same time tugged at one corner of his small, waxed mustache. "And damme, you should know enough about opium. I understand your firm is one of those sending the stuff to China!"

Henry gave him an angry glance. "I do not consider it seemly to talk of business on a social occasion such as this."

Ishbel was surprised that he should be so upset by the mention of De Quincey and the opium matter. She feared the two men might quarrel and so quickly said, "I agree there must be many more pleasant things to discuss than opium!"

Jane at once changed the subject. "You know we have a new monarch now, George the Fourth! By all accounts he is going to be a worse catastrophe than his mad father."

Captain Eric Grant gave another of his laughs. "He is said to be instituting all sorts of economies so he can have more money to spend on his ladies. Rumor has it he means to reduce the size of the army."

Ishbel said, "Will the Duke of Wellington allow that?"

"The Iron Duke?" Jane said with sarcasm. "There's little he can do now. He's lost his power and his popularity. That old man has seen his day!"

Captain Eric Grant demurred. "I wouldn't be too certain of that. He has his supporters still. There is talk he may be included in some post of the new cabinet."

Henry Davis had been sitting in a sort of sullen silence all through this. Now Ishbel turned to him and quietly said, "Is anything the matter?"

"No," he replied. "I'm sorry. I didn't mean to lose my temper just now, but opium is a touchy matter with those of us in the China trade."

"So you *are* involved in the opium traffic?"

"Most of us are," he said with a frown. "We have no choice at the moment. Personally, I deplore it, and I think it only a matter of time before China rebels against the drug imports. Not that I'm optimistic that it will do any good."

She said, "If you consider the traffic in opium immoral, why continue in it?"

"I must or my company would no longer be in a competitive position. Without the opium profits the tea business would collapse."

"You really think that?"

"I do with things as they are. The government ought to pass laws against the drug traffic. But since so many import fortunes are founded on it, I do not expect any action will be taken."

Ishbel gazed at him with concern. "Since you feel so strongly about it, why don't you change to some other business?"

Henry looked shocked. "Our company was founded by my grandfather. It is a family business. Many people depend on it for their livelihood. I cannot just walk away from it."

Ishbel was tempted to ask him why not. But she did not have the opportunity. Their food arrived, and as they all settled down to enjoying it, the conversation became more casual.

The second time Ishbel saw the young tea merchant it was on an afternoon two days later. He came with his open carriage to take her through Hyde Park. He also promised to drive her by Buckingham Palace, the new home of the royal family. John Nash had recently remodeled it under the instructions of King George, and all London was much excited about it.

It was a lovely afternoon, and as Ishbel sat beside Henry in the carriage, she felt at peace with the world. While carriages and horseback riders went by, they passed ponds filled with swans, lovely flowerbeds and rows of stately trees. It was a magical park situated right in the heart of the old city.

She told him, "This is delightful."

"There is much more of London to show you," he promised her.

"I thought I would be homesick for Edinburgh," she confessed, "but London is so full of wonders I have never for an instant missed my home!"

The handsome young man turned to gaze at her earnestly. "Would you consider making London your home?"

"Perhaps," she said, as the carriage jogged along. "But that is not likely."

"Why not?" he asked. "Why not marry me?" Her eyes widened. Despite the fact they had become good friends in so short a space of time, it had never struck her that he would actually propose marriage to her.

"You are joking with me."

"Not at all. I want you to be my wife, Ishbel," he said, reaching and taking her hands in his. "What do you say?"

"Henry!" she protested. "I hadn't expected this."

"You must have known I care for you."

"Yes, but—"

"I'm not given to flowery utterances. I love you and I promise to make you a good husband."

"But we know so little about each other!"

"We know enough."

"And not much time has passed since your first wife's death."

"I know that I want to marry you," he said. "All the rest is unimportant."

"Surely you have not forgotten about her?"

His handsome face took on a strained look. And then he said, "It is not a subject I like to discuss. Let me simply tell you that my marriage to Patricia was not the ideal union all our friends thought it to be."

Startled, she asked, "What do you mean?"

"Patricia was a willful young woman, the daughter of a titled man. She often enjoyed making me miserable."

"Aren't you making too much of that?"

"I think not. Suffice it to say that I am in a frame of mind to desire a happy marriage with you, without any regrets for the past."

Ishbel thought his words a little strange. She said, "And the accident—the one in which Patricia lost her life?"

He frowned. "What about it?"

"You were in the house at the time?"

"Yes. Why?"

"Couldn't you have prevented it?"

"I was in another part of the house. She tripped and fell down the rear stairway."

"I was told that."

"Then why question me about it?"

20

"I'm sorry," she said. "I only wanted to hear your version of it."

"I think we've talked about it enough," he said sharply. Then abruptly changing the subject, he informed her, "In a few minutes we'll be heading for the new palace." And he went on to describe it.

She sat listening with her mind on that mysterious accident still. It was apparently too painful for Henry to dwell on it, so she decided not to mention it again.

Henry proved a persistent suitor. In the weeks that followed he saw her often and never missed an opportunity to try to persuade her to be his wife. When at last she did agree, after a stroll with him one evening, he took her in his arms and kissed her gently.

Then he announced, "We must elope."

"Why?" she asked in bewilderment.

"I think a large, formal wedding would be in bad taste," he informed her. "Many of my friends here would be reminded of my marriage to Patricia."

"We can be married in Edinburgh—in my kirk, which I've attended since I was a wee lass," she told him happily. "You can invite only those of your London friends whom you think will not make you uncomfortable."

Henry's handsome face had become stubborn. "No," he said. "We shall elope and go to Edinburgh on our honeymoon. I want to meet your parents, but that is the best plan. There's a small town just across the Scottish border where we can be married without delay!"

"That is what you really want?"

"It is," he told her. "And when it is all over, you will agree I was right."

Because she was so much in love with him and knew he had gone through a grim ordeal, she reluctantly agreed. One morning they took the early stage from London without even Jane Gray's knowing about it, and they made the long journey to the Scottish border town where their marriage took place among strangers.

They spent their first night together at a friendly little inn on the stage road to Edinburgh. And two evenings later she presented her new husband to her father and mother. When the first shock of their announcement was over, she felt that her parents accepted the situation very well.

Not that it was easy for them. At first her doctor father sat staring at the bridegroom with a worried look on his lined face. His dark hair had begun to gray and ill health had taken its toll of his handsome features, yet Dr. Ian Stewart still possessed an impressive appearance.

He told Ishbel and Henry, "I'm sorry that you chose to run off as you did. I would have liked to have given my daughter a proper wedding."

"It was because of my previous marriage and the tragedy surrounding my wife's death that I did not want a large, public wedding," Henry explained to her father.

Dr. Ian Stewart coughed for a moment in the way that had become chronic with him and then said, "If you feel no guilt in your wife's death, why should it bother you so much?"

Once again Ishbel saw her husband hesitate and actually flinch. Henry said, "I know I acted selfishly. I can only ask you to understand and forgive me."

Standing by her husband's chair, her arm on his shoulder, Ann Stewart looked like an older version of her daughter. Her hair was still its original auburn and she had only a few wrinkles in her face.

Smiling at both Ishbel and Henry, she said, "I do not think we should complain, Ian. I say we are fortunate to gain such a fine young man as our son-in-law."

Dr. Ian Stewart hastened to say, "I have no complaint to make on that score. I only wish we had been consulted."

Ann said, "And now we must have a proper party and introduce you to all the rest of the family."

Henry at once looked uneasy. "It is not necessary!"

Ishbel turned to him with a smile. "I would like it, darling!"

"Very well," he said, but she knew he was not happy about it. His sudden changes of mood were hard to understand.

At her Uncle Walter's insistence, the party was held in the grand ballroom of Stormhaven. Here, where years ago the first Dr. Ian Stewart had introduced his beloved Flora to the family, it was now Henry's turn to be seen and greeted by the many Stewarts.

On the afternoon of the party Ishbel took him on a tour of the grim old graystone mansion. She showed him a portrait of her ancestress Peggy, who had borne a son by the highwayman Black Charlie.

"She was a beauty," Henry said, staring at the portrait with interest.

"She died mad," Ishbel informed him. "She tried to kill my grandfather and grandmother and was herself murdered by a hunchback. And Black Charlie died on the gallows."

"What about their son?"

"He was called Billy and was raised by my grandparents," she told her new husband. "He was a restless, adventurous lad and joined the navy. He sailed with Nelson and was lost at sea in 1793."

"You have an interesting family history," Henry said.

Standing alone with him in the dark corridor, she asked him, "What about you? Are there no skeletons in your closet?"

His handsome face took on a strange expression. Then he

said quietly, "Yes. Perhaps it is time I told you."

"What?"

"My mother deserted my father when I was only a lad."

"I'm sorry," she exclaimed.

"She ran off to Australia with some chap," Henry went on. "My father rushed me off to a school away from London."

"My poor dear," she sympathized, placing a comforting hand on his arm.

"I did not escape the tragedy."

"You were bound to miss your mother!"

"That was not all," he said bitterly.

"No?"

"My father could not bear her loss. He took his own life."

"Took his life!" she gasped.

Henry nodded forlornly. "Yes. One night, after dusk, he went out to a toolshed in the garden and hung himself there. They found his body the next morning."

"How terrible for you!" she said in a whisper.

"They brought me back from school for the funeral," he said in a low voice. "I was not able to cry. I was in a state of shock. Not until I was alone in my room the night after the burial did the tears burst from me."

"Dear Henry!" she said, leaning against him.

His arm went around her. "It was perhaps the worst moment of my life until the business of finding Patricia dead. After his burial I think I became a little mad. I don't remember what happened in the days that followed. Then I was in my Aunt Betsy Davis's house, and it was there I was restored to some sort of a normal life."

"This Aunt Betsy took over your upbringing?"

"Yes. The old woman was good to me. She's still alive and I try to see her regularly. She is a spinster, alone except for her servants and pet cats."

24

Ishbel said, "You must be very fond of her."

"I am," he agreed. "When I was twenty-one I moved back into Number Twenty-Two, Castle Square. And I took over my father's place in the family business."

"That could not have been easy for you."

"I have made a success of the business," Henry said. "And I have come to be fond of the old house once again. I try not to think of my father and what happened in that toolhouse."

"And I had to make you go over it all," she said, in a tone of reproach for herself.

He took her in his arms. "I wanted to tell you. I needed to do it. I have been waiting for the right moment. This seemed to be it."

Ishbel gazed up at him tenderly. "I will be a good wife. I will try to make you forget all those bad memories. Even your unhappy marriage with Patricia."

"You are doing that now, my love," he told her, his lips touching hers.

She was glad they had enjoyed this intimate moment. Later they were taken over completely by the family. The Stewarts turned out in strength for the celebration. Her Uncle Walter was as stern and commanding as ever and looked to be in much better health than her father. Heather Rae, Walter's wife, who had aged a good deal, apologized that neither their son nor their daughter were at home. But bluff Uncle Roger, the shipbuilder, was on hand with his pleasant wife Flo; and along with them came Roger's son Ernest, a young man who had ambitions to learn the banking business, and four-year-old Jean, a merry little girl.

The grand ballroom was brightly lighted, and the fiddlers and the bagpipers played as Ishbel thought she had never heard them play before. All the family friends stood in line to meet her bridegroom. Prominent among them was old Dr.

Jock Gregory, who had just returned to Edinburgh after a visit to Europe. The old man was thinner than in the past, and his brown wig seemed almost too large for him. But he greeted Ishbel and Henry warmly, saying, "I nearly was the grandfather to this girl! But I lost out! Never lucky in love!"

"I'd much rather have you as my friend," Ishbel told him as she kissed him.

"Take your young man off to dance," the old doctor ordered her. "You cannot stand in line all night to be nagged by a lot of dreary old folk like me!"

Happily Ishbel led Henry to the dancing floor, where they made a handsome couple. The music went on, great tables of food were set before the guests in an adjoining room, and the gentry of Edinburgh vowed to each other there had never been a party like it!

It was towards the end of the evening that Ishbel's father was at last able to get her to himself for a few minutes. While Henry was chatting with Walter Stewart, her father drew her aside into a small, unoccupied room off the dining room.

Dr. Ian Stewart's thin face showed a worried expression as he said, "I am worried about you, my dear."

"Why? I'm terribly in love! I have a fine husband!"

"No doubt you are right," he said. "Yet I feel uneasy. I have not been too well. Perhaps that makes me melancholy."

"You must take care of yourself, father," she said with emotion, pressing close to him.

He placed his arm around her. "And so must you," he said in a grave voice. "Since I have always been frank with you, I must be frank with you now. I am not entirely sure about this husband of yours."

Chapter Two

Now, as she stood alone in the garden behind Number Twenty-Two, Castle Square, Ishbel thought of her father's solemn words. Many times they had returned to haunt her. In the beginning she had felt that her father's concern was foolish and needless. But now that seven years had passed since her marriage, she was no longer certain that her father had been wrong about Henry.

It was a frightening thing to distrust your husband, but there was no denying that she had lost much of her faith in this silent, bitter man whom she'd married. The early years in the old house had been pleasant enough. She had been occupied with Will, their first child. Then two years later June had come along. It was natural that the two youngsters should take much of her time.

At first Henry had been delighted with the children, but as he grew more aloof and morose he ceased to show the same interest in them. Things had come to an impasse a few weeks ago when she had quarreled with Henry about his almost ignoring the little boy and girl whom they had brought into the world. As usual, he had stalked out of the house and given her no satisfactory answer. Then he'd returned hours later and had been abject in his apologies, and he had promised to do better.

Ishbel had not been convinced that he meant this. On a sudden impulse she had sent the two children with their governess to stay with her parents in Edinburgh. She wanted to get them away from the tension-filled house that was already beginning to affect them. She also wanted some time alone with Henry to try to discover if their marriage could be saved.

Tonight she had remained up long past her bed time in the hope of talking to her husband, but once again things had gone wrong. She lifted her eyes towards the pale moon just as a dark cloud began to move across it. There was only a small shadow at first, and then much of the moon's surface was cloaked in darkness.

All at once she heard a door close. She swiftly turned to see a shadowy figure emerge from the rear door of the house. It was hard to tell in the near darkness whether it was a man or a woman! The figure apparently saw her; it halted, then turned and made a hasty departure around the corner of the old house. This all happened in a matter of seconds and left her stunned.

The clouds began to leave the moon and the garden took on a magical silver glow once more. She turned and slowly made her way back to the old mansion and let herself in. Her heart was pounding with suppressed fear as she went down the long corridor to her husband's study again. This time the study door was open and she could see Henry seated at his desk. He was holding his head in his hands as if in a mood of extreme despair.

She hesitated and then entered the room, with its walls lined with books, its rose bowl lamp on the broad desk and its heavy-piled carpet. The moment she entered the room she was aware of a familiar odor—the odor of smoke from an opium pipe! And once again she experienced a feeling of terror. It must be true, the thing she'd feared most! Henry had become an addict to the drug in which he so ruthlessly trafficked!

Standing very still and struggling to hide the turmoil inside her, she spoke his name, "Henry."

Her husband lowered his hands and looked up at her. He

seemed in a vague state. His handsome face betrayed no particular expression, but there was a strangeness about his eyes as he fixed them on her. Was it that the pupils were too contracted? Could this be the result of his smoking opium?

After staring at her a few seconds in silence, he said, "Aren't you up very late?"

"Yes. I wanted to see you."

"Oh?"

She studied him closely. "I came here earlier, but you had locked yourself in here."

"You must be mistaken."

"No. I knocked on the door several times and you would not let me in," she insisted.

Henry's handsome face registered patient disbelief. "I'm afraid you're mistaken. As you so often are. I have only just come to this room."

"The door was locked," she said. "I heard voices from in here. Yours and someone else's! You were arguing about something."

"You have a vivid imagination, my dear. It is too bad you couldn't put it to a better use."

"I smell opium fumes in here!"

He smiled coldly. "More nonsense."

"I know the odor."

"I don't deny that," Henry said. "I only deny there are any such fumes in here."

In a taut voice, she said, "You deny everything I say."

"I'm afraid I must."

"Will you dare deny that you have been behaving strangely of late?"

"I do deny it," her husband said in his cool fashion. "I would say it is you who are the one given to strange actions—such as packing the children off to Scotland with their governess without so much as asking my leave."

"I did it to protect them!"

"Indeed. From whom? Me?"

"From your neglect," she said unhappily. "You no longer seem to have any time for them, just as you seem to have no time for me!"

Henry rose from his chair and came around the desk to her. "You are wrong in that and you must know it. I advise that you visit some reliable physician and try to discover what it is that has taken hold of you."

She shook her head. "It is not a doctor I need. I need to regain my trust in you!"

He spread his hands. "Precisely, what have I done to lose your trust? Tell me that!"

Ishbel gave a deep sigh of resignation. "Can you put that question to me? You know all too well how you have been behaving. I feel that I am living in this house with a stranger."

"Nonsense!"

"It is not!" she declared. "Even the servants are hostile to me. Chen lurks in the shadows and spies on me! I hope he gives you satisfactory reports of my conduct!"

Henry registered astonishment. "I do not like that sort of talk. It is obvious to me that you have overtaxed your nerves. You are talking hysterically!"

"I am not," she said. "I'm simply trying to find out what has gone wrong here!"

"Nothing."

"That is not true," she said wearily as she sank down into a nearby armchair. "Who was that who came out of the house just now?"

"I don't know what you're talking about."

"A man or a woman, I can't say which, rushed out of the house and started to run down the garden path. Whoever it was saw me, then turned and fled around the side of the house."

Henry stared at her. "You see a shadow and it becomes a person! Really, my dear!"

"I saw someone," she said firmly. "You will not make me believe otherwise."

"Then that is that," he said. "I shall simply have to allow you to recover from these fantasies as best you can."

"They are not fantasies," she told him. "You had either a man or woman in here with you, and one of you, or perhaps you both were smoking opium."

Henry regarded her with some condescension. "I only wish your parents were here to witness this and hear what you are telling me. What do you suppose they would think?"

She raised a hand to take one of his. He responded to her touch in grim fashion, but she persisted, "Why have you changed so? Why do you rejoice in lying to me?"

"I tell you the truth and you label it lies," Henry said.

"All I ask is that we find what we have lost," Ishbel told him almost tearfully.

Her handsome husband gave her one of his charming smiles. "That is no problem at all. It is entirely in your mind, just as my supposed visitor tonight is."

"I saw someone. I heard someone with you."

"You made yourself believe you saw someone," he corrected her. "That is the truth."

She got up from her chair. "So truth becomes lies and lies are the truth! It will get no better!"

Henry took her in his arms and kissed her gently on the lips. Then he said, "Try to put these fancies out of your mind. They are all that stand between us."

"No," she said. "There is much more! This grim old house with the strange servants you have in it! The ghosts that lurk in the shadows here! The tragedies of the past that refuse to be forgotten! And the wretched trade you are in—trafficking in opium!"

"Go to bed," he advised her. "You are overwrought and don't realize what you are saying. It is not fair to argue with you now. Go to bed. I will come up and join you shortly."

She turned from him and left the room. Her eyes were filled with tears. It had all been wasted effort. He had not listened to her, nor did he intend to. It was as though he were living some new life apart from her, some new existence from which she was shut out.

He left for his office early the next morning before she could have a chance to talk with him. A fog had come in during the night, and now it was so thick she could barely see the trees in the garden. She sat bleakly at the breakfast table thinking of the previous night and wishing that she were with her children in Edinburgh.

The latest word she'd received from her mother was that her father's bronchial trouble had taken on new and more worrisome symptoms. He had been forced to turn his patients over to another physician and seldom left his bed. Ishbel hoped the two lively children might be a pleasure to him and not a burden.

She left the breakfast room and went out to the living room. There she found the housekeeper, the elderly Mrs. Needles, giving instructions about the care of the bedrooms to a new maid. When Mrs. Needles had finished talking to the girl, she sent her upstairs.

Then she turned to give Ishbel her full attention. The old housekeeper had a large, wrinkled face with a protruding lower jaw that gave her a look of grim arrogance. Her yellowish-gray hair was parted in the middle and combed straight back to rest in two skimpy coils at the back of her neck. She invariably wore a shabby black dress with a tiny white apron.

Now Mrs. Needles surveyed her mistress with her smallish, rheumy eyes and asked, "Is there something bothering you, ma'am?"

"Yes," Ishbel said nervously, "there is. Did you notice any strange person enter the house last night?"

"I retire early," the housekeeper said. "Unless special arrangements have been made, I leave it to you and the master to let yourselves in."

"I know that, but I thought you might have heard if anyone was here. You might have noticed the sound of a strange voice."

"I sleep soundly."

"I see," Ishbel said. "I suppose there is no use asking Chen." She knew there wasn't, but she put the question to the old woman to see what her answer might be.

A look of disgust crossed the wrinkled face of Mrs. Needles. "That heathen!"

"What did you say?"

"I called him a heathen, and that is what he is," the old housekeeper said defiantly. "I can scarce go to chapel for having it on my conscience that I work here with a person who worships idols!"

"Chen is entitled to his religious beliefs."

"What religion does he find in a heathen idol?" the old woman asked in an angry tone. "I've seen him up there praying to it. And he won't let any of the maids touch it for fear it might be broken! And him kneeling before it and talking to it like it could answer back while he burns incense before it!"

"Mr. Davis is fond of Chen," she reminded Mrs. Needles. "I'm afraid there is nothing we can do about him."

"And that's a proper shame," the housekeeper replied. "It

would be easier to get help if that Chinaman wasn't sneaking about the house. The girls are so afraid of him they give their notice almost as soon as I hire them."

"You'd best tell that to Mr. Davis," Ishbel said, "though I doubt he'll listen to you."

"Have you heard from the children?" Mrs. Needles wanted to know.

"They are doing very well with my parents."

"A shame to send them away," the old woman complained. "The house needs them!"

"I felt they needed a change," Ishbel said.

Mrs. Needles gave her a knowing look. "I think I know why you did it. You are afraid for them!"

Startled by the old woman's frankness, she said, "Just what do you mean by that, Mrs. Needles?"

The housekeeper came close to her and in a low voice said, "I don't have to spell it out. We both know queer things are going on here!"

"Do you think so?"

"I do and so do you. And I only wondered how long it would take you to find out."

Ishbel stared at the grim, wrinkled old face. "Find out what?"

"That Number Twenty-Two is haunted."

It was not the answer she had expected. She'd been hoping to hear something about the unknown visitors who came to the house at odd hours of the night. Instead the old woman was talking about ghosts.

She said, "Why do you say the house is haunted?"

"Because it is," old Mrs. Needles declared defiantly. "It has been since the master's father hung hisself in the toolshed. That was the start."

"How do you mean?"

"That was the beginning of the haunting," the housekeeper said with a confidential air. "Don't tell me you have never seen him—the ghost of the old master?"

"No," she said uneasily. "I have seen shadows I have not been able to explain. Heard muffled voices below in the night and the sound of doors opening and closing. But I have never seen this phantom you're talking about."

The old woman showed exasperation. "But what you're telling me is the doing of the phantom! It's his shadow you've been seeing, his voice you've been hearing, and it's his moving about opening and closing doors that torments all of us in the night!"

Ishbel stared at the housekeeper. "You honestly believe the ghost of my husband's father is responsible for all the weird happenings?"

"Of course!"

"I'm afraid I can't agree."

"Then you're making a mistake," the old woman said. "You can see what it's done to poor Mr. Henry. He has become real strange of late."

"So you've noticed that also."

"Of course I have," Mrs. Needles said. "I've known him since he was a frightened little lad deserted by his mother. I've seen the change that has come over him, moping about the house as he does now."

"Don't you think it may be something besides his father's ghost that is worrying him?"

"I do."

"What, then?" Ishbel asked tautly.

The old woman glanced about her to make sure they would not be overheard by anyone. Then in a hoarse whisper, she confided, "I don't want that heathen, Chen, to hear me."

"He doesn't seem to be around."

"You can't ever be sure about him," Mrs. Needles said ominously. Then, apparently ready to take the risk, she went on, "I think it's what happened to the first Mrs. Davis is bothering him."

This came as a surprise. "You mean Patricia's tragic death. Her fall down the rear steps?"

"Aye," the old woman whispered. "Her fall down the rear steps. Only I say it wasn't any natural fall!"

Ishbel's eyes widened. "What are you saying?"

"I say that he did it!"

"Who?" she asked, her heart pounding, certain the old woman was about to accuse Henry.

"The phantom," came the triumphant reply from Mrs. Needles. "It was the phantom what done it!"

Shocked, Ishbel stared at the old woman. "Am I to understand that you are blaming the ghost of Henry's father for causing Patricia to fall to her death?"

"Yes."

"Why?"

"Because the old man's ghost knew they weren't happy! He knew that the master was always quarreling with Mrs. Patricia! And so he did her in."

"I find little logic in that," Ishbel heard herself saying.

"Don't expect logic in ghosts," Mrs. Needles said.

She studied the old woman's bleak, wrinkled face. It was the first time Mrs. Needles had ever discussed such things with her directly. In all the seven years she had been in the house, the old woman had not chosen to speak of these things. Yet on this foggy morning she had suddenly chosen to blurt out her strange theories! Ishbel wondered why. Was the old woman telling her these wild stories to cover up real truths? Was it a clever deception on the part of the housekeeper to protect Henry?

36

She said, "What you do stress is that you think the accident which took my husband's first wife is preying on his mind?"

The old woman nodded. "That has to be it."

"If he thinks the ghost did it, as you appear to, why should he feel any guilt?" Ishbel asked.

Mrs. Needles looked wary. "Because he is a very sensitive man. He worries that the ghost did it for him. He blames himself for not getting along with Mrs. Patricia. But then no one could. Not even the mister's Aunt Betsy would come to this house while Mrs. Patricia was alive."

"She doesn't come here now."

"She's old and crippled with rheumatics now," the housekeeper said. "But she used to come around regularly in the old days. Until she and Mrs. Patricia had words."

"What about?"

"The likes of me don't know that," Mrs. Needles informed her. "They quarreled behind closed doors. But I knew they were having a rare battle of it."

Ishbel said, "Why haven't you told me these things long ago?"

"You didn't ask me," Mrs. Needles replied. "I never give information unless I'm asked."

"I see," she said, her mind racing rapidly as she tried to set her thoughts in order. "About the night of Patricia's accident."

"What about it?" Mrs. Needles asked suspiciously.

"Who was the first to find her?"

"That heathen!"

"Chen?" she said. "How did he come to find her when the rest of you didn't?"

"He's always lurking about," the old housekeeper said, as if that explained everything. "I heard the scream and so did

37

some of the maids. But by the time we got there, the master was already there."

"So the second person on the scene was my husband," Ishbel said.

"That's what I understood. When he got there, he found Chen bending over Mrs. Patricia's body at the foot of the stairs."

"She died instantly?"

"Must have. The mister said she was dead before we arrived. He was in a bad state. I hadn't seen him look like that since the time his mother ran off."

"Was he able to take charge?"

Mrs. Needles nodded. "Yes. He called Lawyer Slade in. He's the old man who lives at Number Twenty-Six. He was a friend of Mr. Henry's father. And Lawyer Slade looked after everything from the time he arrived."

Ishbel remembered the ancient Timothy Slade. When she had first come to live in Castle Square Henry had invited the old man over for dinner. She recalled that the white-haired solicitor had impressed her by the little he had said and the way he had studied her. Several times she had caught him at it when she'd turned to him suddenly. Since he held views opposite to Henry's about politics, they had argued about this later in the evening. Old Mr. Slade had not been invited to the house again, nor had he made any attempt to entertain them in return.

Ishbel said, "I rarely see Lawyer Slade these days."

"He has been ill with the gout," Mrs. Needles informed her. "His housekeeper and I enjoy a cup of tea together every so often."

"So he is still at Twenty-Six."

"He'll stay there until he dies, which shouldn't be all that far off," Mrs. Needles said with cold logic. "He has to be over eighty."

"Did he come here often when my husband was married to his first wife?"

"Almost every week he was here for dinner," the old woman said. "But he was younger then. He was also a friend of Lord Carney, Mrs. Patricia's father. Sometimes both Lord Carney and Lawyer Slade would come to dinner."

"I see," Ishbel said with a sigh.

"Mr. Henry was lucky to have Lawyer Slade to turn to that night," Mrs. Needles said, her wrinkled face bleak.

"I'm sure that is true," Ishbel agreed quietly. And she found herself wondering if there might be other reasons besides age and the gout which were keeping the old solicitor from continuing his close friendship with Henry. Was it something to do with that night? Patricia's accident?

Their conversation was interrupted by the cries of a passing fishmonger outside. Ishbel recognized his voice and the ringing cry, which he repeated: "Fresh fish! Haddock, sole, and eel!"

She said, "That is Old Simpson."

The housekeeper nodded. "It is about his time. Do you want fish for dinner?"

"Let us see if the haddock is fresh," Ishbel said as she preceded the old woman to the front door and opened it. Over the past year she had come to know Old Simpson the fishmonger and to enjoy her chats with him. About twelve months earlier he had taken to coming to Castle Square with his pushcart filled with fish. He was a veteran of the navy and proud of the black patch which he wore over his right eye in Nelson fashion.

She opened the door and stepped outside. Old Simpson was just completing a transaction with a servant in the adjoining house. He gave the woman her fish, and she took it inside on a plate which she'd brought for the purpose. The huge old man rolled his pushcart over to where Ishbel was standing and doffed his cap to her.

"Foggy day ma'am," he said in friendly fashion. He had a large frame inclined to stoutness, but it was his face that was most interesting. His nose had been broken, which gave him a battered appearance, and the patch over his right eye added to his rather piratical look. His broad face was weathered and bore many small scars, and his beard always showed a growth of several days. The gray stubble covering the lower half of his face was the final touch. Ishbel had at first thought him an evil-looking man, but now that she'd come to know him well, she liked him.

"It is a foggy morning," she replied in answer to him. "But as an old seaman you must be well used to fog."

"That I am," he said with a chuckle. "And what is your ladyship's pleasure today?"

"What about the haddock?" she asked.

Old Simpson proudly lifted up a fine specimen.

"Caught only last night at the high tide," he said. "I guarantee it to be fresh and tasty."

"Very well," she said, and turning to Mrs. Needles told her, "Fetch a plate and the coins for payment."

"A rare bargain at sixpence," Old Simpson said, beaming at the upheld fish with his good eye.

Mrs. Needles uttered a reluctant grunt of approval of the transaction and vanished inside to get the plate and coins. This left Ishbel and the fishmonger to chat by themselves for a moment.

"Do you ever think of returning to the sea?" she asked him.

The big man shook his head. "Never, ma'am. I served under Nelson. Now that he's gone, none of the others interest me. And I'm too old and used up for any kind of life at sea.

Sixty-one my last birthday."

"Pushing a barrow through the streets is also hard work," she said. "Surely you might find something less irksome?"

"I would like to, ma'am," he said. "But work is not easy to find at my age. And I'm not ready for the workhouse ward for a bit."

"I trust you will never come to that."

"Many have," the big man said. "A poor man has only his health to keep him from misery."

Mrs. Needles came bustling back with the plate. Old Simpson placed the big blue-gray fish on it and took his sixpence. Then with a cheery word of thanks he moved on and began crying out, "Fresh fish. Haddock, sole, and eel!" once again.

Inside Mrs. Needles grumbled, "The fellow doesn't know his place. He talks far too much! None of the other pushcart vendors take such liberties!"

"I find him most interesting," Ishbel said. "He does not have learning, but he is intelligent. And in his navy days he did a great deal of traveling. I'm sure he must have been all the way around the world."

"His fish is no better than the other man's before him, for all that," Mrs. Needles said as she turned to take the haddock to the kitchen.

Ishbel went upstairs and spent most of the morning writing a letter to her parents. She also wrote a special short message for young Will and Jane, which she enclosed in the envelope with the longer letter. Now that her parents were older, she wished that Edinburgh were nearer so that she might visit them more often. She knew it would be helpful to her if she could discuss her concern about Henry with them.

Yet she could not bring herself to put this frightening problem down on paper. She worried that she would only upset her mother and father without managing to convey the real situation to them. She must somehow find an excuse to visit them soon; then, if her father seemed in reasonable health, she would broach the subject to him. With this decided, she sealed the letter and addressed it for mailing.

With the letter in her hand she went to the window of her bedroom and glanced out. The fog was still so heavy she could barely see the most distant part of the half-moon of fine brick houses that faced Castle Square. Old Simpson had vanished with his pushcart. Now a chimney sweep with his ladder slung over one shoulder and accompanied by two little lads (climbing boys, they were called, who did the actual climbing up to clean the chimneys) went strolling by in the heavy mist.

She saw them pass Number Twenty-Six. This brought to mind Lawyer Slade, and she made a decision to visit the old man and have a talk with him that very afternoon. She did not know whether he would receive her or not, but she could only try. Letter in hand, she opened the door to go downstairs and give it to one of the maids for posting.

To her surprise she found herself suddenly confronted by the ancient Chen. He had been apparently standing in the shadows outside her door, listening. Her surprise was followed by anger. "What are you doing by my door?" she demanded indignantly.

The old man lowered his head with the round black cap on it. With his hands crossed inside his voluminous sleeves he said, "I was walking down the hall, missee." He avoided her eyes as he said this, and she knew he wasn't telling the truth.

"You were standing just outside my door!"

"No, missee."

She knew it was useless to protest the matter with him. Perhaps he had been ordered by Henry to spy on her. She no longer knew what to think. Wearily she said, "I'm sure you are lying to me, but it makes no difference."

"Yes, missee," the old Chinese said. He shuffled off quickly to vanish at the end of the hall.

Once again she wondered about Chen and why Henry had so firmly refused to get rid of him. She could not see that he did much about the house. Occasionally he helped in the kitchen, and he attended to the cleaning of Henry's study. These seemed his only duties. With a sigh she continued on her way downstairs with the letter.

The fog continued on through the afternoon. At two o'clock Ishbel put on her bonnet and a warm cloak and set out to make her call on Lawyer Timothy Slade. As she reached the door of the old man's house, she found herself trembling a little. What was she going to say to him? she worried. How much dare she tell him without revealing more than she wished? Hesitantly she lifted the door rapper to announce her presence.

After a short delay the black, panelled door was opened furtively by a very old woman whom she guessed must be the lawyer's housekeeper.

The old woman eyed her with suspicion. "What do you want?" she asked.

"I'm Mrs. Henry Davis, a neighbor," she said. "I would appreciate Lawyer Slade's seeing me for a few minutes."

"He's not practicing law these days," the old woman said tartly, studying her from behind steel-rimmed spectacles.

"This is not a business call," Ishbel said. "I'm here to see the solicitor on a personal matter. He knows my husband well."

The crab-apple face under the laced cap showed no sign of friendliness. But after a moment the old woman said, "You can come in. I'll ask if he'll see you."

"Thank you," Ishbel said politely and entered the dark

hall as the old woman stood aside with the door fully open.

The housekeeper shut the door and hobbled over to a doorway on the left. "In there," she directed.

Ishbel entered the room and found it to be a small living room filled with fine furniture. Its walls were hung with large reproductions of war scenes and the heavy drapes at the windows shut out most of the light seeping in from the foggy day outside. A heavy odor of dampness and stale air pervaded everything.

She heard the old woman's slow footsteps as she ascended the stairway to the floor above. Then there was the distant exchange of voices, voices raised querulously. She stood there in the shadowed room thinking that the voices had a spectral sound, as if they were coming from that unknown world on the other side of death. She gave a tiny shudder. Then she noted the sound of footsteps slowly descending.

A moment or two later the old housekeeper poked her head in the doorway and rasped, "He will see you."

"Thank you," Ishbel said and went out. As the old woman moved to ascend the stairway ahead of her, she told her, "There is no need to show me up. I can find my own way."

The ancient housekeeper gave her a glance of surly disapproval. "I will take you to him," she said, in a tone that indicated she knew her duties.

Ishbel said no more, but slowly followed the old woman as she made her painful ascent. At the head of the stairs there was a large landing and directly in front of them an open door. The housekeeper hobbled over to the door and in her cracked voice announced, "Mrs. Henry Davis!"

Entering the room, Ishbel saw that the old lawyer was seated in a large easy chair with a bandaged foot resting on a footstool in front of him. He was wearing a heavy brown dressing gown and a cravat to match. He was smoking a long, clay pipe, and his wizened face with the thatch of white hair surmounting it looked much the same as when she'd last seen him.

In a reedy voice he apologized, "You will forgive me for not getting up. I'm afflicted with the gout."

"Please don't disturb yourself," she said.

"Sit you down in that chair, Mrs. Davis," the old lawyer said, his pipe still in his right hand. "I can see you better, and it will aid us in our discussion."

"It was kind of you to see me," she said, seating herself in the high-backed chair almost opposite him.

"Not at all," he told her. "Pleasure for me. I don't have many visitors these days. All my old cronies are dead or house-ridden like myself."

"I should have called on you sooner," she apologized. "But I have the two children. Only now that they are in Scotland with my parents do I find myself with any free time."

The old lawyer nodded. "I understand. And how is your good husband?"

She hesitated and giving him a troubled look said, "It is of Henry I have come to speak to you."

A wary look came into the oldster's faded gray eyes. He said, "Of Henry?"

"Yes. I hardly know how to begin. But lately I've been unhappy and I feel that Henry is drifting away from me, that I am losing him."

The old man's eyebrows raised. "I find that interesting."

She leaned forward in her chair. "I hope you may be able to help me. You knew Henry's father as well as Henry's first wife Patricia and her father, Lord Carney."

"So?"

Her tone was pleading. "I hope you may be able to tell me more about Henry—about his earlier marriage to Patricia and the accident that took her life. My husband is becoming a cold stranger! I'm desperate!"

The old lawyer fixed his faded eyes on her. "You say that Henry has changed?"

"Yes. He has become aloof. He rarely talks to me, and when he does, it is usually to reprove me for something."

"Aloof?" The ancient Timothy Slade took a puff on his clay pipe. "I hope you don't mind the odor of tobacco?"

"Not at all," she said.

He said, "You sound almost as if you are frightened of your husband. As if you might be living in fear of him."

"I don't want to admit it," she confessed, "but it is probably true that I am."

Lawyer Timothy Slade's ancient face was solemn. "I wish I could assure you that your feelings are ill-founded. That you are in no danger—" he paused significantly, then added "—but I can't!"

Chapter Three

The old lawyer's grim words confirmed her worst fears. She slumped back in her chair and gazed at the invalid with dismay. Then in a small voice she urged him, "Please go on."

Timothy Slade frowned in silent speculation for a moment. Then he said, "You know that I was a friend of Henry's father and that I also was a friend of Lord Carney and his only daughter Patricia, who married Henry."

"Yes. I know."

"Henry's father was very different from Henry: a large, outgoing man devoted to his business and his wife. But his air of joviality concealed a much weaker inner self than any of us guessed. And when his wife suddenly deserted him and he knew with certainty she wouldn't return, he took his own life."

"Hung himself in the garden toolshed."

"You know the facts? I am all too familiar with them. I was called on that morning, just as I was later called on when Patricia met her death."

"I've heard about your kindness to Henry."

"Kindness? Maybe. I have never considered my motives. I happen to be a man with a strong sense of duty where my friends are concerned. In both cases I felt it was my duty to do what I could at Number Twenty-Two."

"Henry has always spoken respectfully of you."

"Henry had a bad childhood. His mother's running off was shattering enough. But when his father killed himself, it was too much for the boy. His mind went blank for a time, and only sympathetic nursing on the part of his Aunt Betsy

47

restored him to normalcy."

"I knew she brought him up after his father's suicide," Ishbel agreed, "but I had no idea his collapse was so serious at that time."

"The boy was in a bad state. It is my opinion that he still bears the scars of that period on his mind."

Her eyes widened. "You are not telling me you think he might be still a little mad?"

"My experience in the courts has taught me to be most discreet in naming a person mad. I can only say that I think Henry's nature was changed by those unhappy events. And they left him less able to cope with certain problems than the average person."

"That is a statement so cautious I can not quite follow it!"

"I meant to be cautious," the old lawyer said, placing his pipe on a tray on the table beside him.

"When I first met Henry," she told him, "he seemed completely normal. He had the expected moments of sorrow about his first wife's loss, but beyond that there was nothing to make me suspect his mental state."

"You saw him with the eyes of love—the understanding of one who loved him."

"You're saying I didn't see him clearly enough?"

"Perhaps."

She sighed. "Only one person warned me I might be making a mistake. My father."

"He is a doctor, isn't he? Dr. Ian Stewart of Edinburgh, if my memory serves me."

"Your memory serves you well," she said.

"Your father, being a medical man, may have noticed some hints in your husband's manner that a layman would overlook. People in his profession develop an intuition that often is quite dependable."

She smiled wanly. "I thought he was only making the usual objections a father-in-law makes of a son-in-law not of his own choosing. Now I think it may have been more than that."

"You could be right."

"But why did no one else warn me?"

The old lawyer waved a hand wearily. "Few people knew the facts about Henry's private life, and most of them were strangers to you. I, for example, could not go to you with words of caution. But I'm willing to be as helpful as I can now that you have come to me for advice."

She sat forward in the chair again, appealing to him. "But why has this change taken so long in him? We were very happy the first years of our marriage. Now he is a different person. He entertains callers in the night and refuses to admit it. I suspect that he has become an opium addict and the companion of other addicts who visit him in the hours of darkness."

"That is possible," the old man said, "though I hope it is not."

"I pleaded with Henry to give up his tea importing business and look for some other occupation," she worried. "I knew that most of the importers are also involved in the opium trade. But he refused to listen to my pleadings."

The white-haired Timothy Slade said, "That doesn't surprise me. You were asking him to relinquish a family business in which he has great pride. The fact that firms such as his do engage in the opium traffic is not regarded as disgraceful. Many firms of that type are in drugs, and Henry can hardly afford to be an exception."

"It makes the traffic no more acceptable to me," she told him.

"Nor to me," Lawyer Timothy Slade said. "But until there

is a change of thinking on the part of the government, that is the way it will be."

"And if Henry has himself fallen victim to the drug, where is the gain?"

"You may well ask that. Though some contend that opium is not harmful, my experience has been that it brings about a marked change in the personality of the addict."

"And that is what I see in my husband."

"It would be wise not to jump to conclusions."

"When I have entered his study after the departure of one of his night visitors, I have been able to smell opium fumes."

The old lawyer lifted his eyebrows. "That could be damning evidence."

"The house has become an intolerable place," she lamented. "And Henry has that old Chinese, Chen, spying on me. I'm sure of it!"

"Orientals have that rather odd manner about them. He may not be as menacing as you suppose."

"He makes me uneasy. Mrs. Needles, our housekeeper, doesn't like him either. But Henry insists he must remain with us."

"That could be because he was formerly in the employ of Henry's father. A sentimental gesture on your husband's part."

"Mrs. Needles claims that my husband's strangeness dates from the death of his first wife. She thinks he is brooding about the accident that brought about Patricia's tragic end."

The old lawyer looked wary again. "That is a rather strong opinion for a housekeeper to express, and especially to you."

"She has been with the family so long she considers herself one of us."

"That seems likely," he said.

50

"You were there that night? What do you think?"

He considered for a moment. "I should tell you that from the start their marriage was not an ideal one."

"I have heard that hinted by others."

"It is so. Patricia was a high-strung, difficult girl in spite of her amazing beauty. It must have been a terrible shock for Henry when he discovered that she was being unfaithful to him."

"Did he discover that?"

"Yes. He came to me about it in a great state. I tried to placate him, to tell him that we were living in a decadent era with the King himself setting a poor example for his subjects. The scandals of the court were common gossip. It was to be expected that the general morals would suffer."

"Did this make him feel any better?"

"I doubt it. His unfaithful wife brought back the suppressed memories of the terrible ordeal he'd gone through when his mother had played the same game with his father. He kept repeating to me that he would not follow his father's example, that he would not destroy himself."

"At least he was wise in that."

"Yet his manner worried me. I feared he might go to some other dreadful extreme, perhaps try to discover who his wife's lover was and kill him."

"Did he find out the man's name?"

"Not to my knowledge. Patricia somehow managed to keep this from him. Then I worried about something else— that he might decide to kill her."

"And?" she asked, breathlessly.

The old man sighed. "I don't know. It wasn't long after that I was called over there. I found Henry in a state of shock and Patricia stretched out dead at the bottom of the rear stairs. I tried to question him, but he merely babbled. I reported the incident as an accident—though as far as I know, there is no one to say that it was. No witness."

"Chen was on the scene first."

"He claimed he heard her scream and ran to the foot of the stairs. He didn't see her fall."

"Henry was next on the scene. Then the others."

"That is the way it was. After a few hours Henry came back to himself. But I would have to say that he lapsed into a kind of madness for a brief period."

She knew the question she must ask and feared it. But now that she had ventured this far, there could be no turning back. So she asked in a taut voice, "Do you think it a possibility that Henry shoved her down the stairs in a rage?"

His faded blue eyes were sad as they met hers. "I sincerely hope that was not the case."

"But it could have been."

"It could have been."

"And my husband may be gradually breaking under the shadow of his guilt."

"Possibly."

"It has taken this long while, but he might not be able to forget it."

"That could explain the change in him."

Unhappily, she said, "I would rather it be the drug. I cannot bear to think of him as a murderer."

The old lawyer said, "If he murdered, it was done in a moment of madness. I cannot blame the Henry I know for such a crime."

"That makes him nonetheless guilty!"

"True. And worse, it could mean that he might lapse into madness again, and you or your two children could be the victims of his insanity."

It was a shocking possibility she had never heard put into

words before. Now she saw the danger plainly and was thankful she had sent her children to Scotland.

"What can I do?" she asked.

"I fear there is little you can do but watch and wait."

"I'm living in a house of fear," she said brokenly, "a house filled with tragic memories and phantoms of the past. Mrs. Needles insists the sounds I hear of people coming and going are caused by ghosts. She claims the ghost of Henry's father has been seen by herself and others."

"Servants' superstitious nonsense."

"I wonder."

"If you allow yourself to believe in ghosts, you'll truly be lost," the old man warned.

"What can I believe?" she said. "Perhaps my husband did murder Patricia and it is her ghost which is returning to destroy him."

"I would counter that the damage he suffered was done by Patricia alive rather than by her ghost."

"I feel her presence in the house! A menacing presence!"

"You must try to calm yourself," the old lawyer advised. "All this may prove to be of no consequence at all. Henry may recover from whatever is bothering him and become the kind and attentive husband you knew in the days when you were first married."

"If I could only believe that!"

"Henry was fortunate in finding a good and lovely girl like you. You have given him two wonderful children. I cannot believe he will turn against you."

"Thank you," she said. "I need encouragement. He barely talks to me. And I know so little about the past, so little about Patricia."

Lawyer Timothy Slade gave her a strange look. "There is someone actually living in Castle Square who knew Henry's first wife much better than I ever did."

"Who?"

"You may have seen him, though he spends much of his time in Italy. He is back here now. His name is Peter Graves."

"The painter?"

"Yes. You've seen his canvases of rural Britain. And he has been honored with a place in the Royal Academy, even though he is still only about Henry's age."

"I have seen him. He is very tall and stern-looking."

"That's your man."

"I asked Henry about him. I mentioned that a famous artist lived in Twenty-Eight and that it might be nice to entertain him."

"What did Henry say?"

"He became annoyed. He made some derogatory comments about the works of Peter Graves and refused to have him in the house."

"Didn't you think that strange?"

"No. Henry has often expressed his opinions strongly about other artists and composers. He has very definite ideas as to the music and art he prefers."

"There was more to his anger than a dislike of the sort of paintings Peter Graves does," the old man said.

"Really?"

"Yes. Peter Graves was his rival for the hand of Patricia."

Ishbel was astonished. "Henry did not tell me that he had known Graves."

"They're bitter enemies."

"Because of the rivalry over Patricia?"

"That and other things," the lawyer told her. "Lord Carney bought a number of Peter Graves' paintings because of his daughter's interest in the artist. Henry made a number of caustic comments about this in the presence of many of the artist's friends."

"I had no idea."

The old man smiled grimly. "Of course the bad feeling was encouraged by Patricia. She kept the two young men at each other's throats. It gave her a malicious sense of power. The truth was that she didn't care for either of them."

"So it wasn't Peter Graves who became her lover after her marriage to Henry?"

"No."

"Peter Graves could have been no friend of Patricia's after she chose to marry Henry," Ishbel reasoned.

"Surprisingly, he did seem to go on caring for her. Patricia had a great deal of charm despite the evil in her, despite her shallowness. She had the ability to turn men's heads."

"So it would seem."

"If you want to hear another opinion of this, visit Peter Graves and talk to him about her."

"I wouldn't dare. Henry would never forgive me."

"Does he need to know? It might be important to your pursuit of the truth of what happened that night."

Confused, she said, "I have no idea how he would receive me."

"He can be charming," Lawyer Timothy Slade said as he moved about in his chair to ease the position of his gout-ridden leg on the stool. "If you decide to visit him, tell him I sent you. We are friends."

"Thank you," she said. "That might help. But how can I go to him with questions about Patricia without revealing that I'm suspicious of my husband?"

"Simply tell him you'd like to know something about the young woman who was your husband's first wife. That Henry refuses to discuss her with you. At the worst it will seem only a pardonable curiosity on your part about your predecessor."

She saw the cleverness of this strategy and once again was aware of the keen mind of the old lawyer. She rose from her chair, saying, "I have taken too much of your time."

"Alas," he said, with a tired smile, "my time is not valuable anymore. I sit here with my books for long hours every day. Very few come to visit me. Though our conversation has been brooding, the mere fact of your company has given some cheer to a lonely old man."

"Thanks for all your help. I appreciate the way you have taken me into your confidence."

"I sympathize with your position," he said. "I wish I could be of more help. But I'm crippled by this confounded gout!"

Ishbel said, "I trust it will soon be better."

"Thank you. Come back again—any time you think I may be of help."

"Thank you," she said.

"You will forgive me for not seeing you to the door," the old man said.

"Of course," she said. "I can find my own way out."

"Mrs. Holland will be there somewhere to help you," he said from his chair.

She left him and went back down the stairs. Mrs. Holland was waiting in the dark reception hall to open the door for her. She thanked the sour-tempered old woman and went out into the late, foggy afternoon. As she reached the sidewalk, she noticed a carriage draw up before the door of Twenty-Eight Castle Square. A tall, well-dressed man got out of the carriage and paid the driver. Then he mounted the steps of the house, unlocked the door and let himself in. She knew this was Peter Graves and wished she had the courage to go straight to the house and request an audience with him. But she did not feel equal to this yet.

When she reached Number Twenty-Two, she was greeted

by Chen. The old Chinese told her, "Missee Needles in the cellar. In Griffin's room. He is sick."

"Griffin ill?" she said. "It is the first I have heard of it." Griffin was the elderly gardener and man of all work.

"He did not come upstairs this morning, and when Missee Needles went down to him he was still in bed."

"That is too bad," she said. "I must go down and see if there is anything I can do."

She left Chen and took the hall stairway to the cellar. A number of the servants had rooms underground at the rear of the house, each with a single small window, opening at ground level to give a view of the garden.

Griffin's room was near the bottom of the stairway. As Ishbel neared his door, she saw a frightened-looking young maid standing just outside the doorway.

The girl informed her nervously, "Griffin's been taken bad, ma'am."

"So I hear," she said. As she entered the small, cell-like room, she saw that Mrs. Needles was bending over the bed, ministering to the sick man.

Mrs. Needles turned and then came over to her. She said, "It's his heart! He's come out of it, but he's very weak. I say another bad spell and he'll be done for."

"Should I send for a doctor?" Ishbel worried.

"Doctor saw him last time, said there was nothing to be done. He left him some pills. I've given him one and now I'll get him some hot broth."

Ishbel said, "I'd better not disturb him, then."

"I'd say that would be wise, ma'am," Mrs. Needles said. "Mary can stay here and watch. If there's any sudden change, she can call me."

Ishbel told the girl, "Keep a sharp watch on him."

"I will, ma'am," the girl promised, still in a state of awe at being so close to the dying.

Ishbel and Mrs. Needles went back upstairs. In the hall Mrs. Needles confided, "You'd best be thinking about hiring a new gardener. Even if Griffin lives through this, he'll not be able to work again."

"I'll speak to my husband when he comes home," Ishbel promised.

Events then took an unexpected turn. Henry returned home early from the office. Coming to the living room where Ishbel sat with her embroidery, he greeted her with warmth as he had in the early days of their marriage. In fact, he seemed to have recovered all his former good nature.

"I have plans for tonight," he informed her, as he stood before her with a smile on his handsome face.

She put down her embroidery. "What do you mean?"

"I mean we are going out for an evening on the town—if we can find our way in this damnable fog!"

"We have no coachman," she told him. "Griffin has had another of his attacks!"

"Blast it!" Henry said with a sudden frown. "Is he bad off?"

"Mrs. Needles thinks he's very ill. She says we should hire a new gardener and handyman."

"Poor old Griffin," her husband said. "He served both my grandfather and my father. I must go down and take a look at him."

"He is sleeping now," she said. "The best thing is to let him rest. He may be better by tomorrow."

"I'll visit him before I leave in the morning then," her husband said. "And as for tonight, I'll send out one of the servants to fetch us a hansom cab when the time comes."

"I have bought a fresh haddock for dinner," she told him.

"Let the servants have it. They deserve a feast," he said in the same good-natured way. "We shall dine on venison at Westcott's in the Strand. I have already reserved a table and I have tickets for the theater afterwards. Edmund Kean is giving a special performance of Hamlet at the Savoy, tonight only!"

"Kean!" she exclaimed. "I haven't seen him since he went to America on tour."

"He has not been active lately," Henry told her. "He is not well, they say."

"Ever since his divorce and the scandal associated with it, he has been drinking heavily," Ishbel said. "I have been told that he has abandoned himself to a dissipated life."

"His appearance tonight is bound to be one of the few times he will give a performance in London this year," Henry said. "As soon as I heard about it, I made plans for us to attend."

She rose from her chair and told him, "You seem so much more like the Henry Davis I married at this moment. You know, I have been despairing that we would ever know happy times again."

Her handsome husband took her in his arms and smiled at her, "You must forgive my occasional bad moods. I have a heavy burden to carry at the office. Business is not easy these days. I'm sorry if I bring my problems home to you by showing a mean temper." He crowned his apology by kissing her.

She smiled up at him. "You really do want to go out to dinner and the theater?"

"Everything is arranged," he said. "Now hurry and dress in something truly spectacular. I want you to be the best-looking woman at the theater. I want every rake in London to envy me!" And he gave her a playful shove towards the stairway.

In spite of the fog, they managed to get a hansom cab, and with the aid of a lantern on either side of the cab the driver got them to the Strand in time for dinner. It was a merry occasion and the restaurant was crowded. Henry seemed to be enjoying every moment of it all, and he was especially pleased with the low-cut orange gown Ishbel was wearing.

After a feast of venison, accompanied by a fine red wine, they left for the theater. This was also a gala affair. A line had formed at the entrance to the theater, and a husker in a clown costume played his violin for the entertainment of the crowd waiting to enter. Henry tossed the man some coins as they began moving inside with the line.

The crowd cheered when Kean appeared on the gaslit stage. The great dramatic actor accepted the ovation with a dignified bow. When the cheering had subsided, he began his first speech as Hamlet. Ishbel was shocked by his gaunt look. It was easy to see that he was not well. His performance as Hamlet was uneven, but at the best moments he played the part with genius. At other times his voice grew so low that he could barely be heard, and once she thought he staggered slightly as he crossed the stage.

But this was Kean, the king of tragedy, and so everything was forgiven. The performance was, in the overall picture, a distinguished one. The famous actor took many curtain calls, and the audience was still on its feet cheering as he finally left the stage. They seemed unwilling to let him go.

As they made their way out amid the crowd, Henry said to Ishbel, "Kean was obviously unwell tonight. I think his career is at the sunset hour. Everyone sensed that and so were reluctant to see the play come to an end."

"Even sick as he seemed to be, it was a tremendous performance," she said.

"It was," he agreed as he ushered her towards the door

through the jostling herd of people.

Just as they reached the lobby, a tall blond man with a pretty young woman in blue came abreast of them. Ishbel was surprised to see that it was the artist, Peter Graves, of whom she had spoken with Lawyer Slade. This was the second time she had seen him since the discussion about him only a few hours before. It seemed a remarkable coincidence.

Peter Graves glanced at them. On seeing Henry his good-looking face took on a stern look, and he at once turned to the young woman at his side and began talking to her. It was obvious that he had noticed Henry and that the sight of him had not brought back good memories.

Ishbel gave her attention to her husband and saw that the meeting with the artist had also had an effect on him. The look of good humor had vanished from his face, and his brow showed a slight furrow.

Taking her arm, Henry guided her away from the artist and his girl. He said, "I think we can get out more quickly if we take this way."

Actually it was the long way to the street, but Ishbel made no protest. She knew his main purpose was to avoid any further contact with Peter Graves. It was clear to her that Lawyer Slade had not exaggerated the animosity between the two. For Peter Graves and her husband, the late Patricia was still very much a living influence. Their quarrel over the vivacious daughter of Lord Carney was lasting long after her death.

Ishbel soon became aware that the meeting with the artist had marked a dividing point of the evening. From that moment on Henry began to retreat into the shell of aloofness that he had worn so much of late. He hailed a cab, and they slowly made their way back to Castle Square through the fog-ridden streets. She tried to get him to talk as they made the

61

trying journey, but he had slumped against his side of the carriage and mostly sat silently, staring off into space.

The few comments he made were terse and showed his lack of interest in her company. Gradually Ishbel's spirits dropped as the night ended in failure. It was as though she had gone out with one person and was returning home with another. What grim memories had the sight of Peter Graves brought back to her husband, to make him take on this bitter, silent mood once again?

Chen was at the door to let them in. And as Ishbel headed for the stairs, the old Chinese drew Henry aside and whispered something to him.

Henry reacted as if he'd suffered a slap on the face. He stepped back from the old Chinese with a startled look and then nodded to him slowly. Chen turned and vanished in the shadows of the long hall leading to the rear of the house.

From the first stair, she asked, "Aren't you coming up to bed?"

He stood with his top hat and cape in hand, looking uneasy. "In a moment," he said. "I'm going to my study for a short while."

"At this hour? You must be tired!"

"I remembered something. I must write it down or I might forget it again in the morning. You go on up," he said.

She stood there, feeling all the joy of the evening draining from her. Her lovely face was pale as she asked, "What did Chen have to tell you?"

"Nothing."

"Don't lie! I saw your face afterward!"

He made an impatient gesture. "He told me that Griffin was still very ill."

"I don't believe that!"

"Then believe what you like!" Henry said angrily as he

turned and rushed off in the direction of his study.

She hesitated on the stairway, not knowing whether to follow him or not. Then she decided to do so would be useless. It would only lead to more accusations, more quarreling. Nothing to be gained! Wearily she started up the stairs, shocked by the unhappy fashion in which the evening had ended.

The shadows had never seemed more menacing or the old mansion more grim. She made her way to the room she and Henry shared and wearily began to prepare for bed. She thought about the evening and the way Henry and Peter Graves had shown hatred for each other. What strong force still made their hatreds so real?

What sort of woman had Patricia really been? Lawyer Slade had frankly stated that she had been unfaithful to Henry—while the worst Henry had said about his dead wife was that their marriage had not been an ideally happy one. It had obviously been too difficult for him to tell Ishbel the truth: that Patricia had betrayed him, just as his mother had betrayed his father. The scars of that earlier incident were too deep to allow him to cope with his own loss.

Peter Graves, on the other hand, must still revere the dead girl's memory. What had Patricia looked like? There was no likeness of her in this house. If there had been some at an earlier time, they had been taken down and probably destroyed. In his bitterness Henry must have seen that no portraits of her were left. Ishbel could only guess at her predecessor's beauty from the various descriptions she'd been given of her.

Ishbel was in her nightgown now. She moved about the bedroom, turning out all the lamps, leaving only a candle on her bedside table to dispel the darkness of the room. The candle's flickering glow gave the big room an eerie atmosphere.

A good deal of time had gone by, and still Henry had not joined her.

Anger mixed with her grief that her evening should have been thus spoiled. And once again she threw caution aside to leave the bedroom and descend the broad stairway to the lower floor. Moving slowly, like a sleepwalker, she made her way along the dark hall to the door of her husband's study. She tried the door, and once again it was locked.

It was what she'd expected. Now she pressed her ear to the door and there was the vague sound of voices from inside. She could make out neither the voices nor the words being said, but she was certain Henry was in there and he was not alone. It was a repetition of the previous night.

Angered, she pounded on the door and demanded that he come out. There was no response to her cries. She pounded on the door again, with the same lack of results. With a feeling of despair she turned from the door and began making her way back along the corridor.

She moved in the darkness like a ghost. As she reached the bottom of the stairway and groped for the banister, she was suddenly stricken with a chilling fear. All at once she felt she was not alone there in the darkness—that some menacing presence was near her! She found the banister and clutched it and fought her fright as she started up the stairs. She was trembling and had a suspicion that she could hear someone breathing heavily, someone directly behind her!

Then a hand reached out and caught her arm in its cold, clammy grasp. She let out a shrill scream of terror and, summoning all her strength, gave a giant spring forward—and somehow escaped the grasp of the phantom hand!

Having gained this advantage she did not hesitate but raced up the stairs. Reaching the landing breathless and sick with fear, she plunged down the corridor to the door of her own room. Then she swung the door open and quickly slipped inside. She bolted the door and stood pressed against it, sobbing and listening to discover if her pursuer would follow her and try to break into the room.

Nothing happened. Minutes went by. The candle on her bedside table continued to light the room with a phantom glow. She gained control of her sobbing, though she still trembled a little. Crossing to the bed she sat on the side of it and tried to think what it all meant.

What phantom force had she suddenly become aware of when she reached the stairs? Had it been the hand of a ghost that had grasped her so briefly? How had she managed to escape? Had she dealt with the ghost of her father-in-law or the phantom of a jealous Patricia? Or had it been some living person, perhaps Chen? She had never felt the touch of Chen's hand, but she imagined it might be cold and clammy like the hand she had felt on her arm.

Where was her husband? What had summoned him to the study? And who had been in there with him? She wearily slipped between the sheets to consider these questions and wait for him. He would want to know why the door was bolted and she would tell him. Of course he would not believe her, but she would at least make him listen to what she'd gone through.

Her eyes fixed on the candle flame and its constant flickering. She studied its changes of shape and color, lost herself in its magic glow. Her eyelids closed and she sank into a deep sleep.

When she wakened it was morning. Remembrance flooded back to her. She glanced and saw that there had been no one in the bed beside her. The candle had burned itself out. And the door was still bolted exactly as she had left it!

Chapter Four

Ishbel sat up in bed. The bolt still so securely in place on the door told her that Henry had not tried to join her. If he had made the slightest attempt to get in, if he had knocked even once, she would certainly have heard him. She had always been a light sleeper, and with her nerves in the state they had been last night it would have taken even less than usual to waken her.

With a tired sigh she threw back the bed coverings and swung out of bed. She found her slippers and went to the window. The fog had not lifted. Evidently it was to be one of those periods when the fog hung heavy over London for days. She had been told that it was not unknown for the great city to be cloaked in mist for two weeks or more. She had not seen this happen but had been warned of it on reliable authority.

The bleak gray morning matched her own mood. She went back to the bed and pulled the bell cord. It would ring in the kitchen and advise her maid that she was ready for the jug of hot water she always used for her morning ablutions. Memories of the night before began to clamor for recognition. Dinner and the theater seemed a long-ago experience. What remained vivid in her mind was the strange change in Henry at the end of the evening and the phantom attack on her on the stairs!

Had she imagined those moments of horror? Had the clammy hand been a product of her own disordered nerves? She thought not. But what would explain the terrifying happening? Was it one of those eerie events that defied explanation?

She was still standing by the window staring out at the

clouds of fog when a knock came on her door and she heard the thin voice of the maid saying, "Your water is ready, ma'am."

Ishbel crossed to the door and opened it. The tiny girl in maid's uniform came in carrying the big jug of hot water. She placed it on the commode by the china washbasin.

Ishbel said, "Thank you. How is Griffin?"

"Mrs. Needles was down to see him first thing, ma'am. He's having trouble with his breathing. She had permission from the master to call the doctor again. He ought to be here this morning."

Ishbel poured some of the hot water into the basin. "So the news isn't good."

"No, ma'am."

"That will be all, Mary," she said. "I can manage for myself now."

"Yes, ma'am," the girl said and quickly made her exit.

Ishbel was washed and dressed before she crossed to the dresser to find a pin for her dress. It was then she made a strange discovery. On the dresser by her jewel box was a folded piece of notepaper. She lifted up the notepaper and was at once aware of a strong aroma of violets.

Opening the paper, she saw there was a written message on it. She scanned the neatly written words quickly: "Do not pry into the past." The message was signed "P."

She could scarcely credit her discovery. She read the message over, again aware of the strong aroma of violets from the notepaper. Who had left the message there? And why? She was almost certain it had not been there when she came in last night. But could she be absolutely sure? She had been in a distraught state and the light in the room had been poor!

Again she scanned the message, and this time she gave special attention to the initial with which it was signed—the initial of the dead Patricia's name! Was this meant to terrify her further? Had someone written this message to warn her not to try to find out what had gone on at Twenty-Two, Castle Square before she arrived there?

Was it Henry's work? A scheme of his to stop her from badgering him with questions about Patricia's death, questions he must find difficult to answer? She folded the note and placed it in the pocket of her dress. Another strange happening to add to the others.

Downstairs she breakfasted and then sought out Mrs. Needles. The elderly housekeeper's wrinkled face showed her concern over the sick Griffin.

"I don't expect him to live through the day," Mrs. Needles lamented. "And though we've sent for the doctor, there is no sign of him yet."

"My husband gave you permission to call the doctor?"

The woman nodded. "Yes. This morning before he left for his office."

"I see," Ishbel said. So Henry had been in the house. Probably he had remained in the study all night.

"Another death in the house," Mrs. Needles mourned. "It's a place of bad luck!"

"But Griffin is very old," Ishbel said. "Surely his death is to be expected."

"I'm the only one who has been in the service of the family longer," the old woman said.

"What about Chen?"

Mrs. Needles bridled. "I don't count that heathen."

"But you must," Ishbel said. "I'm sure Chen has been here a very long while."

"He came after me," the old woman said with anger on her wrinkled face. "He served the senior Mr. Davis when he was in China for two years, and it was Mr. Davis who brought

68

him back here with him. Better to have left him in his own land."

Changing the subject, Ishbel asked, "Were there any visitors here last night after my husband and I left?"

"Nary a one," Mrs. Needles said.

"How late did you stay up?"

"Later than usual," Mrs. Needles said, "on account of my keeping a watch on poor Griffin."

Ishbel felt she could put it off no longer. She reached in the pocket of her dress and showed the note to the old woman. She said, "I found this on the dresser in my room. It must have been placed there some time last night. Do you know anything about it?"

The wrinkled old face of the housekeeper registered surprise and then awe as she read the message. She looked up at Ishbel and in a strained voice said, "It's in her hand!"

"Her hand?"

"Mrs. Patricia's!" the old woman exclaimed. "It's a message from the dead!"

"Come now," Ishbel said. "I'll not accept that so easily."

"But it is!" the old woman protested. "And the perfume is her perfume!"

"She wore violet perfume?"

"Always!"

"Of course, many people would know that," Ishbel said, taking the note back from the old woman. She tried to sound confident but made a poor success of it.

The wrinkled face of the housekeeper held an awed look. She said, "I don't know what you think about it, ma'am, but I don't like it at all."

"It seems someone wished to play a practical joke on me," Ishbel said, folding the note and placing it in the pocket of her dress again. "But I consider it a joke in the worst of taste."

"When did you find it?"

"Not until just now. But it must have been there from last night."

The old woman gave her an anxious glance. "Maybe it was left in the night."

"By a phantom's hand? Don't ask me to believe that."

Old Mrs. Needles gave a knowing roll of her eyes. "Whether you wish to hear it or not, the phantoms rule this house. Soon poor Griffin will be one of them!"

Ishbel listened to her with amusement. She could not help wondering what the old woman with the superstitious nature would say if she'd heard the rest of her mistress's story. How would she account for the hand that had reached out of the shadows and seized Ishbel? Mrs. Needles would be positive it was another ghostly manifestation.

Because she'd heard enough such talk, Ishbel said no more. Instead she went back up to her room for a while. When the doctor came to see Griffin, they called her down.

The doctor was waiting at the bottom of the stairway when she came down. He was a thin, morose-looking man of middle age who seemed nervous and eager to be on his way. His small black bag was in one hand, and he was consulting his pocket watch with the other. On seeing Ishbel, he hastily put the watch back in his dark blue vest and bowed to her.

"I am Dr. Smith," he said. "I have just had a look at your hired man."

"Griffin," she said. "How is the poor fellow?"

The doctor had a slight frown on his narrow, pale face. "I cannot raise your hopes, Mrs. Davis, I doubt he will last the day. His heart is in poor shape."

"Have you done all you can for him?"

"Everything," the doctor said. "I have left some pills for Mrs. Needles to give him. I doubt they will help. We doctors

70

have not yet learned how to conquer death."

"I realize that," she said. "Thank you for coming, in any case."

"It was no trouble," Dr. Smith assured her. "I had to make a call on Lawyer Slade this morning. He is having a serious spell of the gout."

"I know," she said.

"So I will be on my way," Dr. Smith said in his uneasy fashion. "I have a great many people to see before noon."

"Don't let me keep you," she told him.

After the doctor went on his way, she conferred with Mrs. Needles about the sick man and gave the housekeeper permission to devote her full time to him. With this settled, she went back upstairs for a little.

She read the note supposedly written by the ghostly hand of Patricia and then placed it in an upper drawer of the dresser with some other correspondence. She again noticed the aroma the note gave off and thought about the fact that the scent of violets was the favorite perfume of Henry's first wife. It was someone who knew this fact who had placed the letter there. The first person who came to mind as a suspect was Chen.

Chen had lived in the house with the dead Patricia. Chen was devoted to Henry and would likely carry out any errand he requested. Last night she had surprised the old Chinese lurking just outside her door. Perhaps he had already delivered the note and wanted to get her reaction to it. Or could Chen have worked entirely on his own: copied the handwriting of his dead mistress and found some of her perfume with which to douse the notepaper? It was difficult to know what to think.

Ishbel had always suspected that the old Chinese did not like her, but she doubted that he would set up such a plot against her by himself. It was easier to think of his delivering the message for Henry—particularly if Henry had been responsible for Patricia's death. The object of the note was presumably to warn the second wife against trying to dig into the past and learning the truth.

The incident only served to anger her and steel her in her resolution to learn what was behind her husband's strange moods and what was going on in the grim old mansion. She moved to the window and stared out at the unrelenting fog. Lawyer Slade had agreed to allow her to use his name in visiting Peter Graves.

At first she had thought that she would never do this. But the frightening adventure on the stairs and the arrival of the perfumed note had changed her mind. She recalled the tall blond man from seeing him at the theater on the previous night. There had been a petite, attractive brunette with him. Although he had definitely scowled at Henry, Ishbel did not think he'd looked particularly alarming.

It was this sort of thinking that set her out on a visit to the house of the artist in the mid-afternoon. She approached Number Twenty-Eight with some of the same feeling of nervousness she'd known in seeking out Lawyer Slade. She felt that she must be even more cautious in what she said this time. By all accounts Peter Graves was openly her husband's enemy, and until she knew that her husband was guilty of some crime, she did not wish to betray him.

She was on the steps of Number Twenty-Eight and about to rap on the door when she heard the sound of a cab approaching in the street behind her. She quickly turned to peer through the heavy mist and saw a black hansom cab drawn by a white horse, its driver perched on a high seat at the rear. The cab drew up at the curb before Number Twenty-Eight.

Embarrassed, she stood there as the tall Peter Graves got

out, gave her a curious glance, and then leaned forward to assist the petite brunette who'd been with him at the theater. As soon as the girl was safely on the sidewalk, he paid the driver.

As the cab drove off, Peter Graves made some remark to the young woman. Then he took her by the arm and escorted her up the stairs. He gave Ishbel a questioning look, and almost at once recognition showed on his good-looking face.

He said, "I know you. I saw you at the theater last night."

"Yes," she said, her cheeks burning.

The petite girl stared at her and exclaimed, "Of course! She was with that Henry Davis! You became so angry at seeing him you weren't yourself for a half-hour or more."

Peter Graves told the girl, "We'll not go into that." He gave his attention to Ishbel and asked, "To what do I owe the honor of this call?"

Shyly, she said, "I'm sorry to intrude. I only wish to speak with you a moment. I think you might be able to help me."

The blond man standing in the heavy mist with the petite, dark girl clinging to his arm surveyed Ishbel with a look of contempt. "I'm not sure I wish to help a friend of Henry Davis. And you are his friend, aren't you?"

"I am his wife," she said in a taut voice. "We live at Number Twenty-Two, as you know."

"His wife!" the tall man said with a surprised whistle. "Now that is another matter!"

"I had hoped to find you alone," Ishbel said. "Perhaps I had better return another time." She was certain now that the visit would be a disaster, and she wanted to escape as quickly as she could. She prepared to leave.

"No," Peter Graves said, holding out an arm to stop her. "There is no reason why you should not come inside and state the reason for your call now. May I introduce Doris, my cousin; she is visiting in London at the moment. Later in the day we are attending a tea given by the Duke of Clarendon and his Duchess."

"I don't want to make you late."

"You won't," he assured her. "We have plenty of time. Isn't that so, Doris?"

"There is no hurry," the brunette girl said. "I want to tend to my hair and change my dress for the occasion, so you will have time to talk."

"That settles it," Peter Graves said. He produced a key and unlocked the door. Then he held it open for them and said, "Inside, ladies!"

His cousin went upstairs at once, and the tall man ushered Ishbel into his drawing room. It was much the same size as the one at Number Twenty-Two, and although it was furnished much more plainly, the decor was in excellent taste.

"I pray you be seated," the artist said, indicating a long divan done in white and brown stripes with a frame of finely carved walnut. Feeling that she had made a mistake and was now only compounding it, she sank down on the divan.

She looked up at him and in a small voice said, "I have come here at the suggestion of Lawyer Slade."

"Timothy?" Peter Graves said, standing a distance from her but facing her. "Where does a lawyer fit into this?"

"I went to him as a friend for help," she said. "And it ended with his mentioning your name."

"Mrs. Davis, I must warn you I am a sworn enemy of your husband," Peter Graves said.

"I was given to understand that."

"Then why are you here?"

"Because I am concerned about him. I think he is unhappy about something."

"You two looked happy enough at the theater last night."

"That was an exception. And even that pleasant evening ended in disaster."

The tall blond man looked bored by her words. "I'd think marrying a man like Henry would be akin to a disaster. That was your mistake, ma'am."

She made no reply to this. Instead, she said, "I know that you and Henry were rivals for the hand of his first wife."

"Poor Patricia!" the artist said bitterly. "For all her failings, she deserved a better fate."

"I know very little about her. Henry has told me little. That is why I have come here. To learn something about her. I hope by so doing I may be better able to help my husband."

"I will do nothing to help him!"

"Think of it as helping me, then," she said.

He scowled for a moment, then asked, "What do you want to know?"

"I have found out she and Henry did not have a good marriage."

"So?"

"I also know she was unfaithful to him and somehow he found it out."

"Served him right!"

"Do you know who her lover was?"

"No. And if I did, I wouldn't tell you."

By his tone, she felt that he did know and was simply refusing to say. She went on, "For all you may hate Henry, he has suffered a great deal. His mother deserted his father in a similar fashion while he was a mere boy. It scarred him deeply. And when his own wife gave him the same sort of treatment, it almost sent him into a mental collapse. I feel he is still ill because of it. That is why I'm asking your help. I need to know more about what happened."

A strange look had come to the face of the big blond man.

He said, "In your place I'd be afraid of learning too much."

"What do you mean, Mr. Graves?"

"I mean that in all likelihood your husband killed Patricia by shoving her down that stairway while in a fit of jealous rage."

He had said it. She tried to accept it without too much show of emotion. In a voice with a betraying tremor in it despite her efforts at control, she said, "Isn't that too easy an answer, especially since you admit to hating my husband? The theory that he is suffering from a guilty conscience for his crime fits too neatly. I think there must be more to it."

"I think it is enough."

"I don't think Henry is a murderer."

"Good for you," the artist jeered. "Brave little wife! True to the last! Everyone will give you credit. But you must have discovered by now that many others think the same as I do—that Henry killed Patricia!"

"Did she talk to you often?"

"I saw her occasionally."

"Did she mention Henry's threatening her or tell you that she feared him?"

"We made it a rule never to discuss him when we were together. Patricia had come to understand that she'd made a grave error in marrying him. She made that plain enough. But when we were together, we found other things to talk about."

"If she had left Henry, would you still have been willing to marry her?"

"Yes," the artist said vehemently.

"Despite that other lover?"

"I blamed the liaison on her not being satisfied in her marriage."

"I see," Ishbel said quietly, and at the same time she wondered if he might be bluffing. If, after all, he had been the secret lover.

He took on a sulky mood. "You don't think that?"

"I think you would have been extraordinarily forgiving to take her back."

"I loved her," Peter Graves declared. "That never altered. If she were here now, I would ask her to be my wife."

"Was she very beautiful?" Ishbel asked.

The artist looked surprised. "You have never seen a portrait of her?"

"No."

"Number Twenty-Two had at least a half-dozen portraits of her done by various artists, including myself. What happened to them?"

"They aren't there now."

He began to pace up and down quickly. "Of course! I can tell you what happened to them! He wasn't satisfied with merely destroying her; he had to destroy all her portraits as well!"

"That may be true," she said, "or he may have stored them away so as not to offend me."

"Henry was never that considerate," the artist said with derision. "Our king of the opium trade is not the sensitive fellow that he pretends to be."

"How did Patricia feel about his being part of the opium traffic?"

The artist said, "She preferred to think of him as a tea importer. But that means one and the same thing. Those fine, patriotic, religious gentlemen in the tea trade are all partners in the opium business. Before they are finished they will have us fighting a war with China over it!"

She said, "Do you have a portrait of Patricia?"

He stared at her and gave a harsh laugh. "Would you expect me to?"

77

"You claim that you loved her deeply, that you still treasure her memory."

"I do."

"Then I would expect you to have at least one remaining study of her," she said.

He gave her another of his odd looks. "Follow me!" he said.

She got up from the divan and followed him down a short corridor to the door of another room. As he opened the door, she saw that it was a room with a skylight. In it there were several easels with canvases on them in various degrees of completion. Canvases rested against the baseboards and a number of paintings were hung on the walls.

"My studio," he said, leading her in.

"It is impressive," she said, studying the various paintings. Peter Graves specialized in colorful rural landscapes, and there were many samples of his work scattered about the big room.

"Come over here and take a look," he ordered her. "See this wall!"

She followed him to the other side of the room, and what she saw caused her to gasp. The entire wall was covered with different studies of a beautiful young woman. Some were portraits of her head and shoulders, others showed her in various garb, and one huge painting depicted her resting in the nude on a crimson cloth.

"Patricia?" she said, turning to the tall man.

His eyes were fixed on the various studies. "Yes," he said, in a faraway voice. "Yes. This is all I have left of her."

"She was very beautiful indeed," Ishbel said. And she studied the nearest portrait of the girl, a head and shoulders painting. Patricia was smiling here, and her large brown eyes, pert nose, and generous ruby lips were set in an oval face of great loveliness. The curly brown hair that draped her face and shoulders enhanced the beauty of the young woman to whom Henry had been married.

"Perhaps you understand my feelings better now," Peter Graves said, a somber expression on his face as he gazed down at her. "Your precious Henry is not the only one who was scarred by Patricia's death!"

"Forgive me," she said. "I did not guess that it was such a tender subject with you."

"Well, you've seen her at last," he said ruefully. "I have not destroyed her portraits."

"No," she said quietly. "I can see now that you would never do that."

"Do you think you will remember her?"

She nodded. "It is the sort of face one does not forget."

Peter Graves asked, "Can I be of any more help?"

"No. I'm sorry to have bothered you."

"It doesn't matter. I have nothing against you," he said. "But your husband is another matter."

"I won't bother you again," she promised him. "And I would appreciate it if you'd forget all about my visit. My husband would be upset if he knew I had come here."

"He is not likely to hear it from me. We have not spoken in some years," the artist said.

"I'll be on my way," she told him, and she started out.

He saw her to the door, and as he opened it to let her step out into the fog once again, he said, "I feel very sorry for you."

"Thank you."

"How did you happen to marry Henry Davis, a nice girl like you?"

She shrugged. "I suppose for the same reason that Patricia did. I fell in love with him."

"And now you're as miserable as she was."

"I can't say that," she told him. "I'm worried and puzzled by many things about Henry. Perhaps it will get better. Maybe I've become needlessly neurotic about it all. Being a second wife is not an easy role."

"Being a wife to Henry Davis is bound to be a misery," he said.

"Thank you for the time you gave me," she replied politely.

"I hope you somehow escape this fix you are in," Peter Graves said, sounding as if he meant it.

She went on down the steps without looking back. The door closed behind her. She was still stunned by the display of paintings featuring Patricia. The lovely face was vivid in her mind. And she could not help feeling sorry for the artist who had loved this girl so much that he'd been ready to forgive her anything.

Had Patricia exerted the same fascination on Henry? Was her loss the reason he sank into his dark moods? Had his love for his dead first wife turned him to opium? She felt panic as she envisioned his trying to break the dread drug addiction and turning to a second marriage with herself, a marriage he soon found he could not make a success. Was that the simple answer to it all? That their marriage was a grim charade?

Once again she wished she were back in Edinburgh. Her father would know how to advise her, to prevent her stumbling about approaching strangers for information and humiliating herself. At least her children were safe in Scotland with her parents. No matter what happened to her marriage, she had little Will and June left.

Her eyes were blurred with tears as she hurried across the half-moon sidewalk to Number Twenty-Two. She had learned little from Peter Graves aside from seeing the dead Patricia's face for the first time.

She had no sooner stepped inside the house than she was approached by Mrs. Needles. The housekeeper's wrinkled old face wore an expression of sorrow. Ishbel guessed at once that Griffin must have died.

"What is the news?" she asked.

The housekeeper dabbed a hankie to her eyes and sniffed. "Dead! He breathed his last an hour ago."

"Poor old man!"

"At least he's seen the end of his troubles," Mrs. Needles said. "Should I send for the undertaker?"

"Yes," Ishbel said. "My husband will be home soon to look after the details of the burial."

"Servants who've been with the family a long while are buried in the family plot," Mrs. Needles told her. "The elder Mr. Davis bought sufficient space to give all of us a final resting spot."

"That is good," she murmured, her mind only partially on the matter. "I'll go up and change my clothes for dinner. Let me know when my husband returns."

It was perhaps a half-hour later when the door to the bedroom opened and Henry came in. He seemed in a very somber mood. She was seated at the dresser finishing her hair. She put down the brush and turned to him.

"You know about Griffin?" she said.

"Yes," he replied in a low, controlled voice. "The undertaker just arrived."

"Mrs. Needles claims there is a servants' section in the Davis burial lot."

"There is," he said. He was wearing a black frock coat and gray striped trousers. "We shall have to find someone to replace Griffin."

"I know a man who might be suitable," she said.

"Who?"

"His name is Simpson. He's about sixty and, except for the loss of one eye, he seems in excellent health. He claims to have sailed with Nelson. He comes by here every day with his pushcart selling fresh fish."

Her husband frowned slightly. "I seem to recall your mentioning the fellow."

"He has been most obliging and friendly," she said. "I think he would make a good man of all work."

Henry seemed only slightly interested. He said, "You can approach him about the position if you like. If he is not interested, I will see if I can find someone at the packing house who wants a change of employment."

"Very well," she said. "I shall ask him the next time I see him." She paused and then asked, "Why did you not come up to bed last night?"

He furrowed his brow. "I did and found the door bolted against me."

"You had only to knock and I would have opened the door."

"I did knock."

"I doubt that," she said. "I would have heard you."

"You choose to doubt all I say," was his reply. "What made you bolt the door? You never have before."

"I went downstairs to see what was keeping you, and I had a scare."

"What sort of scare?"

"I'd rather not talk about it," she said, rising from her chair. "You wouldn't believe me, in any case."

"That is typical of your attitude," her husband said. "You come to conclusions without making any attempt to find out the truth."

She faced him grimly. "I went down to see what was

keeping you. I found the door locked again. And I heard you talking with someone in the study."

"The door could not have been locked," he protested. "Why should I lock it?"

"I would like to know that," she said bitterly. "When I was unable to contact you, I started back upstairs. On the way a hand came out of the darkness and grasped my arm! A cold, clammy hand!"

Her husband frowned. "A hand came out of the darkness, you say," he repeated sarcastically.

"I knew it would be a waste of effort to tell you."

"You say a hand grasped you—whose hand?"

"I don't know."

"Then what?"

"I somehow managed to free myself. I raced up the stairs with the feeling I was being followed. When I reached this room, I bolted the door."

"I find that a most unreasonable story," Henry said in his cold, disgusted way.

"I was certain you would."

"And that is your excuse for bolting the door?"

"It was my reason," she said.

"I prefer to think you did it deliberately to provoke me."

"Think what you like."

Henry said angrily, "Haven't we enough problems here without your listening to the servants' tall tales of ghosts and then adding to them in your own way? There are no ghosts in this house!"

"So you have told me."

"It is true!"

She said, "I found Chen lurking outside the door to this room again. I'm certain he was listening and attempting to spy on me."

"More of your imaginative nonsense!"

"You think so?"

"I know it," her husband declared. "You have time and again tried to find a reason for my dismissing Chen. And I tell you now as I've told you before, he stays here!"

She gave a deep sigh. "You say there are no phantoms in this house? What if I can prove differently?"

"You can't!"

"I think I can. This morning I found a note on my dresser, written on perfumed notepaper. It was a warning to me not to delve into the past. And it was signed 'P.' Does that suggest anything to you?"

Her husband's handsome face took on a guilty look. "It does not."

"The perfume on the notepaper was violet. What about that?"

"What about it?"

"Didn't Patricia always wear violet perfume?"

"What has that to do with it?"

She looked at him very directly. "It makes me believe that there is a phantom at work in this house. Patricia's ghost! And that she sent me the note." She was testing him to see what he would say. If he had deliberately planted the message to frighten her, he might reveal it by his reaction.

Henry hesitated and then said, "Show me the note."

She said nothing but went to the dresser drawer where she had carefully put it away. As she pulled out the drawer, she uttered a small cry of annoyance. The sheet of perfumed notepaper had vanished!

Chapter Five

She could not hide her dismay as she turned to him and said, "It has vanished!"

"Vanished?" her husband echoed in a tone of derision.

"There was such a letter! I did not make it up! I showed it to Mrs. Needles, and it was she who identified the perfume and the handwriting as belonging to your first wife."

His expression changed as she told him this. He said, "Are you sure it isn't there? Perhaps you have missed it somehow."

Ishbel saw that Henry was taking her story about the letter seriously now, and she hoped it might also cause him to accept her account of being attacked on the stairway. With a feeling of despair she turned to the dresser drawer again and searched frantically for the missing letter—but to no purpose.

She finally turned to him and said, "I can't understand it. It's gone."

Henry's manner was one of consideration now. He came to stand by her and stared into the open dresser drawer. He said, "In that case, there can only be one explanation. Someone has taken it."

"Who?"

He frowned. "It's hard to say, but unless you have mislaid it yourself, that has to be the answer. Are you certain you placed the letter in there?"

"Yes."

"Well, we'll try to find out about it later," Henry said. "Just now there are more pressing problems. The details of the funeral, for one thing. I have always made it a custom to attend funerals for servants as if they were services for a member of the family. My parents and grandparents also considered this a duty."

"You will want me to attend?"

"I think we should both be there," Henry said.

"When will Griffin's funeral take place?"

"Tomorrow morning. The vicar of St. Mary's will officiate, and burial will be in the Davis lot at St. Mary's Cemetery."

Ishbel listened to this and realized that she would soon be visiting the very grave plot where Patricia was buried; she might even find herself by the graveside of her predecessor. In view of all that had gone on, it would be a macabre experience.

They went down to dinner, and nothing more was said about the missing letter. Henry seemed in a more quiet and considerate mood. He sat before a blazing log fire in the big living room with her and told her of his boyhood days when Griffin had been his friend and confidant.

"In those days he was like a father to me," Henry reminisced. "Griffin was the first one who took me fishing."

"You have never told me of this before," Ishbel said.

"I'd even forgotten much of it myself," he told her. "One becomes so wrapped up in the present, the past fades away. I spent little time talking with Griffin these last few years. I regret that now. I should have let the old man know I remembered his kindness to me when I was a boy."

"I'm sure he understood. He was very good to our June and Will when they went out to the garden where he was working."

Henry's pale, sensitive face showed a sad smile. "He was trying to be a father to our children as he had been a father to me."

She said, "I'm glad the children are in Edinburgh. They

86

have been spared the sadness of his passing. It will not be so hard on them when we tell them about it later."

Her husband gave her a haunted glance. "Death is hard for the young to comprehend. Better to spare them its cruelty until later."

She saw in his face that he was thinking of those other days when as a youth he had been so cruelly exposed to his father's suicide—exposure which had caused him to have a mental breakdown. It was at that time, when he was slowly recovering, that the gardener must have tried to be a foster father to him.

They talked a while longer and then went up to bed. She wanted to talk to him about the missing letter but realized he was in no mood for it. The matter would have to be postponed. The death of Griffin had brought about a subtle change in him. She hoped that he might remain in this new, subdued mood.

That night he did not leave the bedroom. And in the morning he breakfasted with Ishbel rather than going to the tea packing plant early, as was his rule. The fog still hung heavily over the city as they left for the funeral in a rented coach. Another coach carried the senior servants, including Mrs. Needles.

The cemetery of St. Mary's was situated on a small hill behind the church. The vicar was waiting at the open grave. The coffin had arrived ahead of the funeral party and was ready to be lowered.

The gray-haired vicar, who wore a dark cloak over his robe, greeted the party with reserved politeness. The servants gathered around the grave with sad looks on their faces. Mrs. Needles wore a large bonnet that almost concealed her face, but Ishbel saw that she was dabbing at her eyes with a hankie.

The vicar began to intone the short burial service. Henry,

like the other men, stood with head bared and bowed in respect to the dead Griffin. The heavy wet mist made a suitable backdrop for the melancholy scene. The vicar ended his oration and gave a signal to the waiting, bedraggled grave diggers to lower the coffin into the grave and begin filling in the earth.

"A sad occasion," the vicar said in his mournful fashion as he shook hands with Henry and Ishbel.

"Thank you," Henry said. "We will not forget your kindness to us."

"Only my duty, Mr. Davis," the vicar said. "You will excuse me. I have a slight cold and it is very chilly out here." And with a bow he marched off in the direction of the church.

Mrs. Needles came to them and sniffled, "A lovely service! Griffin would have been proud!"

"You will see that the others get safely back to the house," Henry said.

"Yes, sir," the old woman replied. "We're about to walk back to the cab now. It's to be waiting by the church door."

"Very good," Henry said. Then, as Mrs. Needles and the other servants began to walk off into the thick fog, he turned to Ishbel and said, "It is also time for us to leave."

"I'd like to take a moment to look around," she said.

"Look around?"

"At some of the family graves," she said. And she moved a little to the left. "This is the family section over here, isn't it?"

He had returned his hat to his head and now he eyed her with some impatience. "Yes. But this is hardly a suitable time for reading inscriptions and wandering about."

Ishbel halted before a handsome stone of white marble and read the name on it. She turned to him and said, "This is your father's grave!"

"Yes," he agreed, his voice taut.

"And where is Patricia buried?"

He hesitated. "Not here."

She couldn't hide her surprise. "Not here? Surely this is where your wife ought to be buried."

Henry's face had taken on that odd, almost guilty look again. "Let us leave!"

Ishbel did not move. "Where is she buried?"

"Somewhere outside of London."

"Why?"

"It was Lord Carney's wish. He was very broken by Patricia's death. He begged me to allow him to look after all the funeral arrangements and to allow her to be buried in the family vault on his estate."

"And you didn't object?"

"No," he said sharply. "I was quite willing to oblige him in this instance. I do not care to discuss the matter further. Come along!" He seized her by the arm and led her out of the cemetery.

It was a startling finish to the funeral. She had not guessed that Henry's first wife had been buried outside the family lot. It was all very strange. Of course, Patricia and Henry had been at odds, and he had known about her being unfaithful to him. Maybe this had been his way of punishing her after death—banishing her from the family cemetery where she would have ordinarily had a rightful place. Or perhaps, as he had said, he'd allowed the burial to be elsewhere because of the pleas of Patricia's anguished father.

No doubt Lawyer Timothy Slade could tell Ishbel more about this. She would try to talk to the old man again at the first opportunity. But she would have to be careful that Henry didn't find out. She must be certain that Chen did not see her go to their neighbor's house and report it to her husband. Likewise, she must be especially careful if she ever made a visit to Peter Graves again. Henry would never forgive her if he knew she had consulted his sworn enemy, not even if she were able to convince him that she had done it solely for his good.

These were the thoughts running through her mind as she journeyed back to the house in Castle Square after the funeral service. Henry saw her to the door and then continued on to his office in the cab. The old house was cloaked in a somber silence as she entered it.

Mrs. Needles, again in her uniform of black dress and white apron, came to greet her. "Can I get you some tea, Mrs. Davis?" the old woman asked.

"I would enjoy a cup," Ishbel agreed.

The old woman hurried off to get it. By the time Ishbel had removed her bonnet, coat, and gloves and had taken a chair in the living room, the old woman returned with a tea tray and set it on a table by her.

Mrs. Needles poured the tea for her. "It's hard to think of Griffin gone. Poor old man, he went fast at the end."

She took the tea. "Yes. It was sad."

"I could see Mr. Henry felt bad," the old woman said.

"He did. Griffin had been kind to him when he was a boy."

Mrs. Needles gave a nod. "That is true. I remember it all well."

Ishbel sipped her tea. "I tried to find the grave of my husband's first wife," she said tentatively, "and he told me she isn't buried at St. Mary's."

The wrinkled face of the housekeeper took on a wary look. "They took her away. Soon after the accident. They took her right away from Mr. Henry."

"Oh?"

"Lord Carney came. He had a talk with Mr. Henry, and then one of his carriages took her away. None of us saw her after, nor were any of us at her funeral. I hear it was a private one, and Lord Carney had her body placed in the family vault."

"Somewhere outside London, I understand," Ishbel said.

"On the Carney estate," Mrs. Needles agreed. "It was not what we'd expected. Not what any of us below stairs thought was right."

"My husband claims Lord Carney was greatly distressed and pleaded with him to have Patricia buried in this way."

"That may be," the housekeeper said. "But it doesn't seem right."

"Something else," Ishbel said, looking up at her. "The letter I showed you, you remember?"

"The one from Mrs. Patricia with the perfume?"

"Yes. I put it in my dresser drawer to show my husband, and it disappeared."

Mrs. Needles jaw dropped. "Disappeared?"

"What do you think of that?"

The look of astonishment on the wrinkled face was replaced by one of grimness. "I'm not absolutely surprised," the old woman replied.

"You're not?"

"No!"

"May I ask why?"

"Simple enough, ma'am. I'd say the letter was stolen."

"By whom?"

Mrs. Needles showed disgust. "Who do you think, ma'am? You shouldn't have to ask me! By that heathen! That Chen!"

"You think so?" Ishbel said, not very satisfied. She might have known the old woman would at once accuse Chen. And this was disappointing, since Ishbel had the feeling that Chen had nothing to do with it.

"That Chinaman is always stealing," Mrs. Needles said

with anger. "He takes things from the kitchen all the time."

"This was a rather different sort of theft," she said. "Why would he want that letter?"

Mrs. Needles was nonplussed for a moment. Then she said, "I don't know, ma'am, but I suspect him!" It was not at all a logical comment.

Their conversation was interrupted by the sound of the fishmonger calling his wares outside. Ishbel at once remembered that her husband had given her permission to speak to the old man about taking over the post of the deceased Griffin. So she told Mrs. Needles to go to the door and invite the fishmonger in.

Ishbel went to the reception hall to greet the big man with the black patch over his right eye. When Mrs. Needles held the door open for him to enter, he came in and removed his cap.

Ishbel said, "Perhaps you have heard that our gardener-handyman has just died."

The big man with the grizzled beard nodded. "Aye, ma'am. That would be Griffin."

"Yes," she said. "We need someone to fill his post, and I thought of you. Does the offer interest you?"

The broad, weathered face of Simpson showed pleasure. He said, "I'm flattered that you would consider me, ma'am."

"The salary would at least be as adequate as what you derive from your fishmongering," Ishbel said.

"No fear of that, ma'am," Simpson said. "I only worry that I might not do the job as well as Griffin."

Ishbel smiled. "We're quite willing to chance that. If you take the job, you will have free quarters in the cellar and all your food here."

"I consider it a rare privilege," Simpson said. "I know a little about gardening and I'm not afraid of driving the coach.

If you will give me a few days to dispose of my fish business, I'll be glad to accept."

Ishbel was pleased. It would mean she'd have someone in the house on whom she could depend, someone who would give first allegiance to her. She said, "You may have the time you need to turn over your present business. When you arrive, Mrs. Needles will show you your room and give you a list of your duties."

The big man smiled his gratitude. "This is a rare moment for me, ma'am," he said. "I wish that all Nelson's veterans might find themselves blessed with as good an opportunity."

"I consider myself lucky in getting you," Ishbel told him.

The big man clumsily thanked her again and went on his way with his fish cart. Mrs. Needles closed the door after him looking somewhat less than pleased.

She grumbled, "He didn't take long to accept."

"It is a rise in the world for him. Don't you think he'll turn out well?"

Mrs. Needles shrugged. "I wouldn't like to say at this time, ma'am. You only know how capable these people are after you employ them. Griffin was a hard worker even in his old age."

"I have an idea Simpson will give his best to the job," Ishbel said, at the same time thinking that the advantages of having someone in the house whom she could trust implicitly would more than balance any shortcomings Simpson might have as a gardener.

"Is there anything else?" Mrs. Needles asked.

"Yes," she said. "As soon as luncheon is over, I want you to send Chen out on an errand. I have a call to make and I want to be sure he isn't spying on me."

"I'll send him to the greengrocer's," Mrs. Needles said. "He prides himself on being able to pick out good vegetables, though I can't say he does better than anyone else."

Shortly after the noon meal, Mrs. Needles sent the black-suited Chen off to the greengrocer's. As soon as the old Chinese was out of the court, Ishbel put on her cape and cloak and hastily made her way to the home of Lawyer Slade at Number Twenty-Six. The fog still cloaked the city, and it was cooler than usual for the time of year.

The old man's housekeeper greeted her more cordially on this second call and showed her in to see the old man without delay. Lawyer Slade was apparently feeling better. He'd made his way downstairs with the aid of a walking stick and was seated in a tall-backed chair in his study.

The white-haired solicitor waved her to a chair opposite him and, gazing at her across his desk, said, "I'm pleased to see you so soon again."

Blushing, she replied, "I didn't want to bother you. But when Griffin was buried this morning, I found out something I didn't know before."

His wizened face showed interest. "What was that?"

"That Patricia was not buried in the Davis family lot in St. Mary's Cemetery."

"I could have told you that."

"It seems very odd to me. Also, Henry became angry when I tried to question him about it."

Timothy Slade sat back in his chair. "You have not met Lord Carney yet?"

"No."

"He is a very forceful man," the old lawyer said.

"I have gathered that from what I've heard of him."

"He is an old friend of mine."

"I know."

94

"But I will not attempt to conceal his faults. In his youth he was a rake. He and George were boon companions, and he made many a trip to Brighton with the Prince Regent."

"I had the impression he was very stern."

"He is now," Lawyer Slade chuckled. "Grim reformation seems to be the inevitable condition of most rakes in their declining years. Lord Carney has become deeply religious and upright."

"So?"

"Patricia's death was a sore blow to him. He was dedicated to this only daughter, and he never quite approved of Henry Davis as her husband. So when she met with her accident, his lordship came here and insisted that she be buried in the family vault on his estate."

"I'm surprised that Henry allowed it."

"You forget that Henry and Patricia were not on friendly terms at the time of her death. Henry could have created a scandal about his wife's behavior if he had wished. As you know, he kept it quiet; because of the failure of his parents' marriage, he was determined to preserve a facade of respectability for his own."

"I can understand that."

"Nevertheless, he had presumably come to hate Patricia for betraying him, and so it was not terribly hard to turn her body over to her father."

"But surely that act alone would tend to create gossip," she said.

"Lord Carney played the role of distracted father to the hilt," Lawyer Slade said. "So it did not appear unreasonable for Henry to give in to him in this regard—even though Henry knew the true reason for his father-in-law's making such an unusual request."

She felt a recurrence of that chilling fear again as she ventured, "You mean that Lord Carney suspected Henry of murdering Patricia?"

"Yes."

"I wonder that others did not pick up the notion and create more gossip."

The old lawyer showed a smile on his wizened face. "This did not happen because Henry had been discreet about his wife's unhappy behavior. He had kept it to himself except among his most trusted friends. I was flattered that he included me in that group."

"Peter Graves knew about it."

"You went to see him?"

"Yes. And I had my first glimpse of portraits of Patricia. He has a host of them. She was a beauty."

"No one could deny that. As to Graves' knowing, he would have heard the story from Patricia. They continued to meet secretly up until the time of her death."

"Could he have been her lover?"

"Not at the time of her death," the old lawyer said. "He undoubtedly was earlier."

"So you do not think this business of Patricia's being buried elsewhere has any real bearing on whether or not Henry might have caused her death."

"That is correct."

She sighed. "Peter Graves minced no words in calling him a murderer."

"I'd expect that. Still, I think Peter is allowing his passion for the late Patricia to blind his judgment. I know as much about the matter as anyone, and I'm inclined to think Henry is innocent of any wrongdoing in his wife's death."

Ishbel sighed. "I wish I could be sure of that."

"How is he behaving?"

"He was better last night, but this morning he seemed to

retreat into himself again. He shuts me out of his thoughts, rushes away from me."

"Something is troubling him."

"I know," she said. "If I could learn what it is, I might understand the true situation." Then she told the old lawyer about finding the perfumed letter and its disappearance.

Having listened to her he said, "Someone wants you to stop asking awkward questions."

"Who?"

"Most likely the murderer," the old lawyer said, "assuming that Patricia was murdered."

"Eliminating Henry, who else could be guilty?"

"Many people. Her lover, whoever he was. Peter Graves is even a possible suspect. It would not have been hard for him to get into Number Twenty-Two and have a quarrel with Patricia. He might have asked her to abandon her new lover and return to him."

"I hadn't thought of that."

"You should," the old man told her. "Peter Graves has a wicked temper. If Patricia did refuse to turn to him again, he would have been capable of murdering her."

"Perhaps I was wrong in going to see him."

"Not necessarily. At least you now know what Patricia looked like."

"I'm terrified that Chen spies on me and reports to my husband," she added. "I had Mrs. Needles send him off on an errand before I dared to come here and see you."

"That is a difficult situation," the solicitor agreed.

"I don't know which way to turn!"

"Perhaps if you let time take its course . . ."

"Wait and see, is what you're saying. What is to happen to me in the meantime?"

The old lawyer said, "I can only tell you what I feel. I

cannot make you believe that I am right."

She saw the sense of his argument and, rising from her chair, said, "Of course you are right. I have allowed my panic to take over my good sense."

"One cannot blame you for that," he replied. "You came to London as a stranger, filled with trust in your husband. It is not easy to learn that he may not be what you at first felt him to be."

"You have been more than kind," she said.

"I wish I could do more," he sighed, gazing down at his gout-ridden foot unhappily, "but you see how it is with me."

She was about to leave when she remembered to tell him about hiring Simpson. She explained, "I feel I shall be able to rely on him in case of an emergency."

"Excellent," the old lawyer said. "It will serve to put you at your ease."

She went back to Number Twenty-Two, Castle Square in a better frame of mind. Just being able to talk to someone was helpful. The thick fog was persisting and looked as if it might go on for days more.

Mrs. Needles was waiting to greet her, and at first Ishbel worried that Chen might have returned ahead of her. So she asked, "Is Chen back?"

"No," the old housekeeper said. "We have been lucky in that. But you do have a visitor."

"A visitor? Who?"

"A Mr. Ernest Stewart from Edinburgh. He is waiting for you in the living room."

"Cousin Ernest!" she said, in a tone of pleased excitement. "Of course! I remembered in my mother's last letter she spoke of his coming to London!"

She hurried past the old woman and entered the living room to discover a tall, good-looking young man waiting for her there. He was wearing a traveling coat of brown that matched his hair and bronzed complexion. He was a sturdy type and stood a good head taller than herself.

"Ernest!" she exclaimed with delight. "What a pleasant surprise!"

The young man lifted her up and kissed her. With a jolly laugh he said, "I promised you would be the first person I would visit when I arrived in London, and here I am."

For a moment all Ishbel's fears were forgotten. She basked in the warmth of the reunion with her cousin Ernest, now grown to a handsome manhood. She exclaimed, "You must live here with us while you are in London!"

"I'm afraid I can't do that," he said. "I've taken lodgings with another young man at the bank. I'm here in London representing the family firm with the British Merchantile Bank. It is a big responsibility."

"Your Uncle Walter must think you ready for it, or he would not have risked your taking the post. He is extremely cautious."

"I hope I can live up to his expectations," Ernest said.

"Do sit down! And take off your coat! I must hear all about what is happening in Edinburgh!"

Ernest removed his coat and threw it on a nearby chair as he sat on the divan with her. He said, "First, let me say your youngsters are enjoying their stay with their grandparents."

"I hoped they would."

His handsome young face shadowed a trifle. "On the debit side, your father's bronchial trouble is definitely worse. He is in poor health, but his spirits are good."

"Is there any hope he will be better?"

"Dr. Jock Gregory, who is an expert in lung diseases, is worried about him. But he is trying out a new treatment and thinks it may offer him some improvement."

Ishbel said, "Dr. Gregory must be over eighty now!"

"Eighty-four, to be exact," Ernest said with a smile. "And he is still active at the medical school of the university. A remarkable man."

"He once courted Grandmother Stewart," she reminded the young man.

"And he has outlived both grandmother and grandfather. He is very fond of your mother. He calls her a devoted nurse—and she is that to your father."

"Poor mother! I hope the strain is not too much for her."

Ernest said, "She never complains and she looks very well. But Aunt Heather is bedfast with some sort of internal trouble. They don't expect her to last long."

"That will be hard on Uncle Walter," she said. "But then he has always been deeply occupied with the bank. That will help sustain him if he loses her."

Ernest nodded. "I'm certain of that. He misses James, who now has his own plantation in North Carolina. I think the fact that his son chose not to go into the bank was a sore blow to him."

"It was the same with my father when he chose to be a doctor," Ishbel said. "That is how Uncle Walter came to head the firm."

"James has a son, according to the latest word, and I hear his wife is expecting again."

"So both of Uncle Walter's grandchildren will be citizens of the United States. I'm sure he would rather see them grow up in Scotland."

"Perhaps he will advance the plan to James. But I doubt it will do any good. James is happy with his American wife and enthusiastic about the prospects of the Southern States."

"How is your father?" Ishbel wanted to know.

"First rate—and expanding the shipping firm all the time.

He is determined to make Roger Stewart Shipping as important a name as Stewart Banking."

"And why not? Especially since he has always appeared to enjoy his work so thoroughly!"

"Dad is a happy man," Ernest agreed. Then he paused and asked, "How is Henry?"

She at once was brought back to the present with all its problems. Quietly she said, "He is doing very well. But his business takes a great deal of his time."

"London is a metropolis of world trade," Ernest said with enthusiasm. "I shall get great training here."

"I'm sure of it," she said.

"I must be going," Ernest said, rising and putting on his coat again. "Give Henry my best regards and tell him I'm sorry I missed him."

"I will," she promised, also getting to her feet. "You must come to dinner with us soon."

"I'll let you know when I have a free night," Ernest promised. "I have to do some traveling back and forth to Edinburgh for a while, so it is difficult to name a definite date."

"Let me know as soon as you can," she begged him. She linked her arm in his as she went to the front door with him. "You can't imagine how happy your visit has made me."

On the steps, he asked, "Is it always this foggy in London?"

"Not always," she said, "but we've had a siege of it lately."

He bent to kiss her on the cheek again. "I shall be back to see you often. It is good to have one of the family here in London."

Ishbel remained standing in the open doorway until her cousin Ernest walked off far enough in the fog to be lost to sight. Then she closed the door and sighed deeply. Ernest had spoken a greater truth than he'd realized when he'd said it was good to have a fellow member of the family in London. She was deeply grateful that he had come to this city where she had married and made her home. With things so desperate for her, it was comforting to know Ernest was not too far away.

When Henry came home for dinner, she told him, "Ernest is here in the city. He's representing Uncle Walter's bank."

Her husband raised his eyebrows. "I hardly thought him old enough for that."

"He is only twenty-one, but apparently he has considerable ability. Otherwise, Uncle Walter wouldn't have sent him here."

"I'd hope not," Henry said. "He'll be up against the smartest bankers in the world here in London."

"I asked him to come to dinner."

"When?"

"A date wasn't set. He has to make several trips back to Edinburgh before he settles down here permanently. He said he'd let me know when he was free."

Henry said, "What was the news from Edinburgh? How are the children?"

"Well and happy," she said, and she went on to tell him all that Cousin Ernest had told her. Henry listened but did not seem deeply interested. She sensed he was in one of his aloof moods.

Almost as soon as dinner was over, he excused himself from her by announcing curtly, "I have brought back a heavy batch of invoices to go over. The ship sails tomorrow, so I must check them tonight. I shall be in the library."

"Very well," she said with polite resignation. This routine on his part was becoming all too familiar. She suspected that once she was upstairs and safely out of the way, one or more of his mysterious callers would arrive.

But she was too weary of their pointless quarrels to make any protest. She went on upstairs to their bedroom with the thought of going to bed early. When she reached the door she found it open, and Chen was standing in the middle of the room with a guilty expression on his sallow face.

She asked, "What are you doing in this bedroom?"

The old Chinese in the black round cap and black silk suit stood uneasily with his arms folded and his hands thrust into the ample sleeves of the black silk jacket.

"Someone rang the bell rope," he said, indicating the cloth bellpull by the bed. "I came in answer to it."

"And found no one here," she said scathingly. She did not believe his story and felt this to be another instance of his spying on her. She told him, "I do not need you here. You are dismissed from any duties you may have had up here!"

"Yes, missee," he said with a bob of the ancient head with the black, round cap. "But the bell did sound. Who could have rung it?"

She knew what he was hinting: that the bell ring had been activated by a ghostly hand, that he had been summoned there by a phantom.

She was equally certain that he was making up the story to frighten her and to account for his being in the room. Somewhat angrily she said, "I do not wish to discuss the bell ring! Please get out of this room!"

"Yes, missee," Chen said and soundlessly glided across to the door and out.

She began to think that Mrs. Needles was right, that it was probably Chen who had placed the perfumed letter on her dresser to terrify her, and that later he had removed it from the drawer where she had placed it to show her husband.

In a depressed mood she remained in her room as darkness came. With the heavy fog the night turned dark more quickly. She lighted a lamp on the dresser and then made up her mind to go downstairs and complain about Chen. She made her way down the shadowed stairs to the silence of the floor below.

She went directly to her husband's study door and found it closed. She tried the handle, and it was locked. She placed an ear against the door and managed to hear a murmur of voices from inside. One voice was clearly Henry's; the other seemed to be that of a woman. She could not hear what was being said.

She knocked on the door several times without getting any answer. She decided bitterly it was just the same as before. It was then she formed a plan. Henry's caller would be leaving the house soon. Why not hide somewhere outside the front door so she could see who it was? As long as Henry felt she was safely upstairs, he would not hesitate to allow his visitor to leave by the front door.

Ishbel found a dark cloak and went out into the cool, misty night. There was an entrance to the servants' quarters under the front steps. It was reached by going down steps to below the street level. These steps were located on the left of the regular steps. She went down them, and this provided her with a hiding place. When her husband's caller emerged, she would be able to get a good look at the person without being seen. She pulled the cloak about her more tightly, shivered a little from the cold and from her fears, and began her vigil.

Chapter Six

Ishbel waited under the front steps in her secret hiding place for a long while before she was rewarded by hearing the door open above. Her heart began to pound relentlessly and her whole body went taut. No words were being said, but she heard the sound of the door closing and then light footsteps coming down the steps.

Despite her fear she forced herself to emerge from her hiding place so she might see who it was. As she came up the side stairs, she saw that it was a female wearing a dark cloak with an attached hood, something like the one she herself had on.

"Wait!" she commanded the woman.

The woman turned to her with a frightened glance, and Ishbel's blood ran cold—for she was staring into the face of the dead! The lovely, terrified face she was facing in the fog was the face of the dead Patricia, Henry's first wife!

The woman made no reply but ran off into the foggy night. Ishbel ran after her, but it was a hopeless pursuit. She lost the phantom figure almost at the start and was left bleakly alone in the thick mist a short distance from Castle Square, not knowing what to think.

Suddenly she was aware that she was not alone any longer. A tall figure loomed up in the fog beside her, and she heard a familiar voice say, "What are you doing out here alone on a night like this?" It was the artist, Peter Graves.

"You!" she said in a weak voice with a tremor in it.

"Did I frighten you badly?" he wanted to know.

"I was frightened before you came along," she said with a tiny shiver.

"I should think you would be," the artist told her. "Don't you know that dippers and bludgers are lurking in the fog and waiting for prey on nights like this?"

"Dippers and bludgers?" she gasped.

"You don't know the underworld slang," Peter Graves said with good-natured disgust. "I'm talking about pickpockets and burglars!"

"Oh!" she said.

"And you're all too likely to be taken for dollymop!"

"A dollymop?"

"A servant girl doubling as a street walker, if I must explain," the artist said. "Don't they teach you anything at all in Edinburgh?"

"I'm afraid I've led a sheltered life."

"It's not apt to continue that way now you're married to Henry Davis," the artist jeered.

"Please!" she said unhappily. "I must go back."

"I should think so," the artist said. "You will otherwise get in trouble here. I'll see you to your door."

"No!" she protested. "Henry will be outraged! He doesn't even know I'm out of the house!"

"Now, that's interesting," Peter Graves said, taking her by the arm. "Let me inform you, however, that I'm not afraid of what your Henry might think or say."

Reluctantly she allowed him to guide her along the foggy, dark street towards Castle Square. She was trembling badly and did not know what to say to him. At last she decided.

She said, "You can leave me a little distance from the door."

"I'll take you to it," he said. "Even if your precious scoundrel of a Henry should be on the doorstep waiting for you, he'll be hard put to recognize me in this thick fog."

"It is good of you."

"I have no grudge against you. Only your husband."

She said, "I had a shocking experience just now. I was standing outside our house and I saw a ghost leave it."

"A ghost?" he echoed mockingly. "What sort of ghost?"

"The ghost of Patricia. I saw her face plainly. Unfortunately, when I called out to her, she ran off into the fog and I lost her. That was when you came along."

The young artist had halted and now he was staring down at her. "Do you realize what a monstrous story you are telling me?"

"I'm only telling what happened."

"It's preposterous! Patricia is dead!"

"I recognized her from your portraits of her!"

The tall young artist was silent for a moment. Then he asked, "How did you come to be out watching?"

"I knew Henry had a visitor. He was locked in his study with her. It has happened before. And always there is an odor of opium smoke left in the room. Tonight I stationed myself outside so that when she left I would have a look at her."

"And you saw Patricia?"

"I swear it!" she declared. "I just had a brief look at her, but it's not a face you could mistake. She gave me a terrified glance and then ran from me!"

Peter Graves stood there in thought. Then he said, "You made some sort of mistake. It must have been some other girl who resembled Patricia."

"How could another resemble her so closely?"

"I don't know," he said. "But one thing we do both know is that Patricia is dead."

She gave another tiny shudder. "I wonder."

"Wonder what?"

"Whether she's dead."

"Explain yourself."

"Suppose she wasn't killed in that fall, only badly injured. Her father took her body away for a private burial. Perhaps she recovered in his care and is seeing Henry on the sly again."

"It's a fantastic theory," the artist said. "But even assuming that it is true, why should she behave in this fashion?"

"The smell of opium," Ishbel said knowingly.

"The smell of opium?"

"Yes. Perhaps Patricia had become an opium addict. That might have accounted for her tumbling down the stairs. It could be that old Lawyer Slade mistook her drug coma for her being dead. It might even be that Lord Carney took her away at the point of death but she did not die. And it is her returning that has made such a change in Henry! He is not only faced with a drug-ridden first wife he presumed dead, but he has made himself a bigamist! My marriage to him could be illegal!"

"Damme!" Peter Graves said with a touch of awe in his voice. "You have more imagination than any female I have ever known!"

"It may all be true!" she worried.

"I don't believe any of it for a moment," the artist said. "If Patricia were alive and in trouble, she would come to visit me, not Henry."

"How can you be sure?"

"Because I knew her well," Peter Graves said. "You saw one of Henry's other females and mistook her for Patricia. You were in a bad state of nerves. If there were the slightest resemblance you would magnify it."

"So I made a stupid mistake," she said bitterly. "That is all there is to it."

"A reasonable error, not a stupid mistake," he corrected her. "Now let us leave poor Patricia asleep in her grave, and

I'll see you safely home." He began to walk again.

"I still think I saw her," she protested.

"Think what you like."

She said, "I would expect you to be concerned. You went to the length of calling my husband a murderer on little or no evidence. And now you won't allow me to believe what I saw with my own eyes."

In a surprising change of manner, he said in a weary voice, "I wish most heartily that Patricia were alive. I miss her more with every passing week. But the story you offer me is too fantastic."

"Life can be fantastic! The unexpected does happen!"

"Not in this case," the artist said.

"How can you be so certain? You claim you knew all about Patricia, yet I suspect there was much you didn't know—the name of her last lover, for instance."

His step became brisker. "I do not know his name. I did not consider it in good taste to query Patricia on such matters."

Ishbel felt she had won a point. "So there were many things you did not know about her!"

"I know the most essential thing," he said sharply. "Patricia is dead!"

"I'm not so sure," was her reply.

They had reached the door, and she saw there was a faint glow of light coming from one downstairs window. She told the artist, "That is Henry, still in his study. With a little luck I may be able to get inside without his ever knowing I was out of the house."

Peter Graves returned to his jeering tone to say, "I wish you luck! Take my advice and stay off the streets at this time of night. It might be more dangerous next time."

With that he doffed his top hat briefly and then turned and

109

marched off into the mist. She was left standing before the front door uncertainly. After a moment she summoned all her resources of courage and boldly made her way up the steps. She tried the door and it opened easily. With a deep breath of relief she let herself in. Then she hurried to the stairway and made her way up to her room. She was undressed and in bed before Henry finally joined her. She pretended to be asleep as he prepared for bed, extinguished the lamp and took his place in bed beside her.

She dared not move for fear she might betray that she was awake. So she lay in an awkward position until the sound of his regular, heavy breathing indicated that he was asleep. Then she turned on her back and stared up at the ceiling through the dark shadows.

In spite of Peter Graves' scoffing at her theory, she still was of the opinion she had seen Patricia, living or dead, and living or dead Patricia could mean nothing but trouble for herself and Henry. How much did Henry know? How deeply was he involved in the plot, whatever it might be?

She was tormenting herself with these questions when she finally fell into an uneasy sleep. It was a sleep riddled with dreams in which she confronted the dead Patricia over and over again. These tormented dreams made her twist and turn restlessly. When she wakened in the morning, she felt as if she had not slept at all. Henry had already risen and dressed. No doubt he was either having breakfast or had finished it and was already on the way to the office. She lifted herself on an elbow and pulled the bell rope. Then she lay back with an aching head to wait for the maid and the morning jug of hot water.

The fog had lifted slightly, and a bleak sun was attempting to show itself over London. She had barely finished breakfast when Old Simpson arrived with all his worldly goods in a sack tied around the middle that he carried in one of his powerful hands.

"I'm at your service, ma'am," said the huge old man with the black patch over his right eye.

"I'm glad you've come," Ishbel said. "Mrs. Needles will show you to your room in the cellar. Then she'll take you on the rounds of the garden, the toolshed, and the stables."

"It won't take me long to get the knack of things," the big man said. "This is a fine chance for me, and I intend to make the most of it."

"I like your attitude, Simpson," Ishbel smiled. "When you have finished your tour of the place, I will talk with you again."

"Very well, ma'am," Simpson said as he was led away by a grim Mrs. Needles.

Ishbel went directly to her room and at once sat down to write a long and informative account of what she had experienced and endured since coming to the house in Castle Square as Henry Davis's wife. She made certain allegations in the letter that she felt sure would solve one or more of the mysteries which she'd been faced with. In its way, the letter was a combination confession and will.

She asked in the letter that if she should die of some unexpected sort of accident, her death should be thoroughly investigated. Then she wrote another letter to her children and sealed it. She wrote on both envelopes that they were to be withheld until the event of her death. Then they were to be given to her parents and her children respectively. With both letters sealed and ready she went downstairs with them and sought out Simpson. The big man was standing in the garden, surveying it gloomily.

"There's a deal of work to be done out here," he said, studying the numerous flower beds with one good eye.

"But it need not be beyond you," Ishbel said.

"I can manage," the big man said.

"I want you to," Ishbel told him seriously. "I need someone here on whom I can depend."

Simpson eyed her strangely. "I'm not sure I understand, ma'am," he said.

She bit her lower lip. "I'm afraid I can't really explain, except to say that there are times when this old house frightens me."

"Yes, ma'am," he said, looking puzzled.

She handed him the large envelope with her two letters in it. "I want you to take this. Inside there are two letters, one for my parents in Edinburgh and one for my children. In the event I should have an accident that proves fatal, I'd like you to send them on for me."

He looked at the package. Then he said, "I'd call that morbid thinking, ma'am. We couldn't do with that in the navy. Live for the day was our motto—and Nelson's! Nothing is going to happen to a fine young woman like yourself!"

"I hope not," she said. "But this is a precaution in case of the unexpected. It will ease my mind to know that the envelopes would be sent."

"Then you have my promise I'll send them if the need should arise," the big man said solemnly.

"Thank you, Simpson," she said gratefully. "And not a word of this to anyone! Not even to my husband!"

"Very well, ma'am," Simpson said. "I'll take the package to my room at once and hide it away."

Somehow the former sailor's promise eased her mind. In her letter to her parents she had said all the things she had formerly held back. In the event of her death they would know that she had strong suspicions concerning her husband. She had no doubt they would react quickly to the letter and see that a full investigation was conducted of her demise.

Nothing of event took place during the next few days. Ishbel began to wonder if she hadn't been too hasty in coming to conclusions, if perhaps her fears of the old house and of her husband were groundless and should not be entertained.

Simpson proved an excellent choice as a handyman. He went to work with enthusiasm and put in long hours in the garden. Even Henry had to admit grudgingly that he was an excellent worker.

Watching from the rear living room window, her husband said, "He's turning out very well for a fishmonger! I didn't think it possible."

"I'm certain he'll be all right," she told Henry. "He has much more strength than Griffin, and so the work isn't as hard on him."

Henry glanced at her with a half-smile. "You wanted him, didn't you?"

"Yes."

"So you've had your way," her husband said. "You should be satisfied."

"I am, very much satisfied," she said.

Henry then surprised her by asking, "What about your cousin Ernest?"

"I have not heard from him since he paid me that call."

"No doubt he has been busy adjusting to his new position and the city."

"I'm sure that is it," she agreed. "When I hear from him again, I'll find out when he can come to dinner."

"Yes. Do that. I'll enjoy meeting him," her husband said. He was much more agreeable to the idea than he had been earlier.

Ishbel began to believe that things had taken a change for the better. She was on the point of writing Edinburgh and asking that the children and their governess return. But before she could do that, two things happened to upset her.

The first incident took place on a lovely warm night. The weather had taken a decided change for the better following the spell of fog, and London was enjoying marvelous summer weather. On the night in question Henry had retired to his study to do some work, and Ishbel was left to stroll about the house in a rather lonely mood.

She studied the garden from one of the rear windows, and it looked so good to her she decided impulsively to throw caution aside and go out into it alone. As soon as she stepped out into the warm night air she felt better. Simpson had been busy with the gardens, and in the moonlight she could almost identify all the brilliantly colored blooms.

Before she knew it, she was a fair distance from the house. Then suddenly she spotted another figure in the garden. A dozen yards or so ahead of her she saw the dark cloak of a female lurking by the bushes to the left of the gravel path.

The sight of the motionless figure standing there touched off a sensation of fear in her. Until that moment she had been in a relaxed mood. Now her body went taut, and she gazed ahead at the cloaked figure with frightened eyes. Was this a return of the phantom she'd seen that night in the fog—the phantom Patricia who had vanished in the mist?

She stood there with her eyes fixed on the figure and her heart beating violently. She was waiting for the shadowy female to make some move, but this did not happen. At last her curiosity began to balance her fears. And very slowly she made her way along the path to the spot where the cloaked woman was waiting.

Her tension increased with each step she took towards the mystery woman. At last she found herself within a yard or two of it and discovered she'd been the victim of a cruel hoax.

There was no woman—merely a cloak with a hood draped craftily on a tall bush to create the illusion of a person lurking there.

Indignation followed on relief as she asked herself who had done this. Someone must have suspected that she was going to take a walk in the garden alone and had placed this booby trap out here to scare her! She was thinking all this when she heard a footstep behind her and knew more surprises lay in store for her.

She was about to wheel around and see who it was when she was seized by powerful hands. She had a chance to scream out just once before the strong hands circled her throat and began to crush the breath from her! She clawed at the cruel hands without result and then found it easier to give up and fall into a velvet blackness which had nothing to do with the night.

Then someone was shaking her. She did not want to wake up. She moaned and tried to escape those hands. But she was unable to halt this stirring back to awareness. She opened her eyes and saw that someone was bending over her as she lay stretched out on the grass. It was Chen!

"Missee!" Chen exclaimed in distress.

"What are you doing here?" she asked weakly.

"Missee screamed. I was standing on steps at the back of the house and heard you. When I came running, I found you on the ground!"

She wearily lifted herself on an elbow. "Did you see anyone else?"

"No, missee. Just you!"

"But there was someone else! A man attacked me!"

"Saw no one," Chen said, returning to his stolid manner.

She struggled to her feet, her head reeling and a kind of nausea rising up in her. Her neck burned from the choking she'd received. She traced the sore circle with her hands.

Now a new figure came striding towards them from the shadows. It was Simpson. The big man with the eye patch came to her and asked, "You all right, ma'am? I heard voices down here."

"I had an unhappy experience," she said. "Chen came to my aid."

Simpson gave the bent old Chinese a grim glance. "I had an idea he might be bothering you."

"Nothing like that," she hastened to say, fearful that the burly ex-seaman might decide to pounce on Chen. She turned to the old Chinese and said, "Will you please go summon my husband?"

"Yes, missee," Chen said with a bob of his black-capped head. He trotted off towards the house.

Simpson glared after him and then asked her, "Are you sure he wasn't giving you some trouble, ma'am?"

"Quite sure!"

"I don't trust him. Always sneaking around. He comes up on you before you know he's anywhere near! Heathen Chinee!"

She saw that he was adopting Mrs. Needles' prejudice against the old Chinese. She told him, "You mustn't take too much stock in what Mrs. Needles says. She seems to dislike Chen without having any solid reason for it."

Ominously, the big man said, "I'd say you could find good reasons without too much trouble."

She was relieved when a moment later she heard Henry's voice in an exchange with Chen's. And then the tall figure of her handsome husband came towards them. He at once came to her and took her in his arms.

"Chen says that someone attacked you. He found you out here on the grass unconscious!"

"For only a moment," she said.

Henry asked in distress, "Were you hurt badly?"

"No I'm going to be all right. My throat aches a little, that's all."

Henry turned to Simpson. "How did you get here?"

The big man explained, "I heard voices. When I came to see what was going on, I found the mistress and that Chen out here."

Ishbel said, "That was after Chen roused me."

"I heard nothing," Henry said. "But then I was in the study with the door closed."

It was at that moment she began to suspect that her husband might have been her attacker. He could have swiftly made a circuitous route through the garden on hearing Chen's approach. While the old Chinese was busy trying to revive her, it would have been easy for Henry to continue on back to the study. Then when Chen came for him he could show surprise and concern. It could have happened that way. The cruel hands on her throat might have been those of her husband. But she prayed that this mightn't be so!

"What brought you out here?" Henry asked, breaking into her reverie.

"It was such a lovely night," she faltered. "And I was lonely. I only planned to venture out a few steps to get the air."

Henry asked, "Then what brought you way down here?"

"I saw someone," she said. "Or thought I did."

"Someone? Who?" Henry wanted to know.

"A woman in a cloak and hood. Just beyond here. But it was a prank played on me. As I came closer, I saw that it was only a cloak carefully draped on a bush."

"Where is it?" Henry asked.

"There," she said, pointing to the bush.

Henry went over by the bush and then turned to her with some impatience. "There's nothing draped on this bush that I can see."

Startled, she crossed to where he was standing. To her dismay, she saw that he was right. There was no cloak draped there. In a small voice, she said, "I don't understand it!"

"Probably another of your imagined phantoms," Henry said with such annoyance that she began to tremble.

She was frightened not only because of what had happened but because she was beginning to think that Henry was the one behind it. She insisted, "There was a cloak there!"

"It's gone now," Henry replied.

"I can't deny that," she said lamely. "But I must go on insisting that it was there. Deliberately set out to draw me into a trap."

Simpson spoke up in his rough voice, "Someone might have put the cloak there to divert attention. Maybe some burglar was ready to make a raid on the house when the mistress came out and caught him by surprise. When he heard Chen and me coming to her help, he snatched the cloak from the bush and went back up over the rear fence to the street beyond."

Henry did not seem to appreciate the comments of the big man. It was clear he resented his intrusion in the matter as he told him coldly, "Thank you for your views, Simpson. And now we do not need you any longer."

The big man looked abashed. "Yes, sir," he muttered and he turned and went up the path towards the house.

"He was only trying to be helpful," Ishbel said.

"I do not need his help," her husband said with anger. He turned to Chen, who had been lurking in the background, and said, "Chen, see my wife safely back inside. I'm going to take a look around here and see if there are any signs of the wall being scaled."

"I can wait here," Ishbel said. "It isn't safe for you to be alone out here. If there was a burglar or burglars, they may still be hiding somewhere nearby. They could come back and attack you."

"I'm willing to take that risk," was his reply. "Go along with Chen."

She knew there was no arguing with him when he was in one of these moods. With a sigh she turned, and she and Chen walked back to the rear door of the old mansion. Along the way she speculated that Henry might be giving his show of independence because he knew he was in no danger. If he had been responsible for the incident, he could bluff it out in this manner without concern.

Back in the house she waited in the reception hall for Henry's return. He was not out in the garden long. As she heard his footsteps coming down the hall, her heart began to pound harder. She wondered what sort of story he might offer her and whether he would try to twist things around so that the blame for it all would be on her.

Henry came into view and halted before her with a frown on his sensitive face. He surprised her by announcing, "I owe you an apology. I think all you said was true."

"Of course I told you the truth," she exclaimed. "What would make you think otherwise?"

"It was a far-fetched story. You must admit that," he chided her. "But I found evidence that someone had climbed over the wall. The light ironwork mounted on top of the wall has been broken away in one section, and the vines on the bricks are torn down. The ground by the wall also indicates the impact of feet. We have had an intruder tonight!"

Ishbel at once accepted this as truth and pushed aside all the suspicions she'd felt about him. She did this because she wanted to and because Henry seemed convinced that he had made an important discovery.

"What will you do?" she asked.

"Inform the police," her husband replied at once, further allaying her suspicions. "You will repeat your story for them."

"Do you think they will be of any help?"

"I very much doubt it," Henry said with some bitterness. "There are those who claim that since Sir Robert Peel organized the Bow-Street Runners into a regular police force there has been less crime in London. I am one of those who remain skeptical. In spite of the numbers of new bobbies and detectives, crime continues."

"Surely the police must have done some good," she said.

Henry shrugged. "We'll notify them in the morning and see what they do for us. If they find out who scaled the wall and attacked you, I'll look on them more favorably."

"By tomorrow I doubt if the intruder can be traced."

"I question that," her husband said. "At any rate, we shall see."

Ishbel was tempted to ask him why the police should not be sent for at once. Knowing his tendency to sudden anger, however, she decided she had better let him do it the way he liked. At least he was going to have the police investigate, and this was more than she had hoped for.

The detective did not arrive until late the next morning. He was a stout, friendly man with a ruddy face and sharp blue eyes beneath gray eyebrows. He was wearing a rather shabby brown coat and trousers of a matching shade. He bowed to Ishbel when Mrs. Needles showed him in.

"I am Detective Hawker," he told her. "Your husband came by the station and gave us an account of what went on here last night."

"It seems we had an intruder," Ishbel told him.

"So your husband claims," the stout man said dryly, as if that fact alone did not convince him. "How is your throat this morning?"

"A little sore, that is all."

The stout man gave her a warning glance. "You can consider yourself lucky. Once those fellows attack you, the chances of your coming out alive are small. They feel they might as well hang for murder as for burglary."

"I was saved by the servants' hearing my scream and coming out to help me."

"They frightened your intruder off," Detective Hawker filled in helpfully.

"I suppose so," she said uncertainly.

He gave her a sharp look. "Your husband didn't report the crime to us last night."

"No."

"Why?"

"Did you ask him when he gave you the report at the police station this morning?"

Detective Hawker hesitated. "I did not take the report, but there is no explanation in the information I have here."

"Then I'm afraid I can't help you," she said.

"I think it strange that he didn't come to us at once," the stout man said.

She sighed. "To be frank, my husband has a rather poor opinion of your new police force. I think he would like to see you fail in what you've come to investigate."

Detective Hawker's fat face registered surprise. "But you were attacked! You might have been killed! Whatever his feelings about the police, his concern for you should come first. He ought to have come to us directly last night."

"I felt that. But I also tried to accept his reasons for not doing so."

The stout detective said, "We encounter a lot of hostility, some from the very people who should be most interested in what we are trying to achieve."

She bowed her head and studied her folded hands in her lap. "I'm sorry I can't be more helpful," she said.

Detective Hawker smiled. "Don't dismay, ma'am. I'm sure we'll get along. Would you be kind enough to show me the garden?"

"Of course," she agreed. "Come along."

Now that she had risen, she realized that he was a short man, no taller than she was. He had obviously bowed legs, and he was broad of shoulder as well as of stomach. She judged that he had been a policeman in the not too distant past and was enjoying his elevation to being a detective.

As they stepped outside, he said, "Pretty garden! You're Mr. Davis's second wife, I understand."

"That is so," she agreed, taking him along the gravel path.

Simpson was working at a flower bed a distance away. He looked up at them and then busied himself with his work again. Detective Hawker gazed at him with interest and asked, "Who is that?"

"Our gardener. His name is Simpson. I will vouch for him. He is most trustworthy. He and Chen were the servants who came to my aid last night."

"That black patch over his eye—it looks familiar. But I can't place him!"

"Perhaps you saw him on the streets when he was a fishmonger. He used to go about with a pushcart."

"Of course!" Detective Hawker said with delight on his fat face. "Simpson the fishmonger. That's where I saw him."

She led him to the bush and said, "The cloak was draped here. I came close before I found out it wasn't a real person."

"And then you were attacked?"

"Yes."

Detective Hawker's sharp eyes fixed on her. "You were ready to accept that there might be a female here in the garden. Why? Had you seen a similar figure lurking here before?"

Uneasily she said, "I think I might have."

"You must know," he insisted. "Had you seen a cloaked woman in or around the house on some other night?"

She didn't answer him at once. She knew that in the end she would have to be truthful with him. She said, "On several other occasions I saw and heard a mysterious woman in the house and outside it."

"Did you inform you husband?"

"I did."

"And?"

"He suggested I was mistaken. That the woman I saw was a figment of my imagination."

"But you didn't accept that?"

"Not really," she said. "I think my husband may have known who the woman was. I am nearly certain she was his visitor."

Detective Hawker lifted his eyebrows. "You surprise me. The first Mrs. Davis died in the house here as the result of a strange accident, didn't she?"

Ishbel's cheeks crimsoned. "She fell down the stairs and broke her neck. I don't think there was anything strange about it."

"I see," Detective Hawker said, as if this didn't satisfy him. Then he added, "I'll take a look at that wall, if I may— the spot where the burglar is supposed to have made his entry."

"Yes," she said, and led him over to the place. The sky was

cloudy, making the day coolish. She shivered as she stood waiting for him to examine the fence. She saw that the ornamental ironwork on the top of the brick fence was bent at this point, jammed down so that anyone coming over it would not be caught by the sharp iron spikes that were there for protection as well as for ornament.

The detective examined the ground carefully at the spot. He also found the torn vines and held them in his hands. Then with an agility remarkable in one of his girth he raised himself up to the top of the fence and gazed down at the other side of it. When he had finished all this, he came back to Ishbel with a strange look on his round face.

He said, "There may have been someone come in over that fence last night; then again, maybe not. There should be more marks on the ground on the other side. It almost looks as if somebody deliberately did all the damage on this side to make it seem there was an intruder." He studied her with his keen eyes. "It could have been an inside job."

Chapter Seven

Ishbel heard the stout Detective Hawker's announcement with a feeling of dismay. She feared the same thing! But she did not dare reveal her feelings and let him know that she suspected her own husband.

In a small voice she said, "That's most frightening."

"I would find it so in your place," the detective replied as he glanced back at the wall again. "I find the situation there a trifle too pat. There is the suggestion of staging."

"I see."

Those sharp eyes probed her once again. "Another thing: I do not like the delay by your husband in reporting the crime."

She had felt the same way; in fact, she had spoken to Henry about this very thing. His excuse had been that he did not think the police would be of help in any case.

She said, "My husband is a self-willed man. It is often hard to follow his thinking."

"So it would seem," Detective Hawker said without taking his eyes from her. "You appear to be extremely nervous. Is there anything you haven't told me?"

She began to feel panicky. "No, nothing of consequence," she replied at once.

Detective Hawker sighed. "I see. Well, I shall talk to your servants and then make a report of all this. I can't promise results, but we will do the best we can."

"I'm sure you will."

"You didn't get even a brief glimpse of your attacker?"

"No."

"That makes it more difficult," the stout man told her. "If

there is anything which comes to mind later, don't hesitate to look me up. You can find me at the police station."

"I'll remember," she promised.

He stood there solidly planted on his bow legs and looked back in the direction of the old mansion. "I've been told this house has a dark history—that your husband's father killed himself here and that his ghost is reported to haunt the place."

"It is a familiar legend," she said.

He eyed her again. "Have you ever seen the ghost?"

"Not to my knowledge."

"Ever experienced any strange events, unexplained knocks, phantom footsteps or ghostly voices?"

She hesitated. "That is hard for me to say. Old houses like Number Twenty-Two are always filled with strange sounds."

"You are a cautious woman, Mrs. Davis," Detective Hawker said with a hint of irony in his tone.

"I'm not especially aware of it."

"Your husband's first wife met with a mysterious death. I have no doubt they'll be saying her ghost returns to the house also."

"Perhaps," she said in a taut voice. "Legends grow over a period of time." She was thinking about her own experience in seeing Patricia. She wanted badly to tell him about it, but she couldn't find the courage to do so.

"I'll talk with this Simpson first," the detective said, "and then we can question Chen."

"Very well," she said.

Detective Hawker plodded across the garden on his bow legs and began to question Simpson. The big man remained on his knees by the flower bed at which he was working. Ishbel thought there was a certain hostility on the part of the gardener towards the detective, but Simpson answered all the questions put to him in a terse fashion. When the detective finished questioning him, Simpson at once returned to work.

She then led the detective inside. Chen was summoned from the kitchen and also questioned. The old Chinese was polite and prompt with his replies, but his testimony did not add up to anything new or important. When Detective Hawker completed his questions, he turned to Ishbel and said, "I must be on my way now. But remember, I shall always be at your service. If anything else comes to you, or if you are frightened by anything, do not hesitate to call on me."

"I won't," she said gratefully.

It was not until the detective had left that she began to reproach herself for not being much more frank with him. She had allowed him to leave without confiding her dark suspicions about her husband. But he had surmised something from her manner; she was positive of that. The detective was a wily old man, and she was of the opinion they had not seen the last of him.

She felt a need to get out of the grim house. There was a short street of shops not far from Castle Square. It included a milliner's and a store that combined yard goods with a supply of ladies' furnishings. She needed some new ribbon for a bonnet and she was looking for material for a gown. This seemed a good time to take care of the errands.

She changed into a print dress and selected a suitable parasol before embarking on her shopping excursion. Mrs. Needles met her on the stairway as she was leaving and she told the housekeeper where she was going.

"I won't be gone long," she promised.

The old woman gazed at her sympathetically. "I wonder that you are able to go out at all, considering what happened last night."

"I want to try to forget it."

"We all want that," Mrs. Needles lamented. "Such a dreadful scandal! To have the police visiting the house!"

"We had no alternative but to call them in," Ishbel told the old woman.

Mrs. Needles gave a nod of agreement. "I realize that, but I say it's a dark day for us all! There's no telling what is likely to happen!"

Ishbel left the house with this rather dramatic declaration ringing in her ears. It almost seemed that old Mrs. Needles was more troubled about the Davis servants' losing their respectability in the Square than about the miscreant who'd attacked the mistress of the house. Perhaps Mrs. Needles also had her own dark thoughts as to who the criminal might be.

Ishbel put up her parasol against the strong sun of the midday and started along the sidewalk on her way to the nearby street of shops. But she had proceeded no further than Number Twenty-Six when a heavy rapping on a windowpane caught her attention and made her halt.

Peering out from under the parasol, she saw the wizened face of Lawyer Slade in a window of the second story of his house. He was beckoning for her to come up and talk to him. She at once closed her parasol and mounted the steps of Number Twenty-Six. Apparently the old man had called to his housekeeper, for the door was opened at once.

The ancient housekeeper said, "He's waiting for you upstairs."

"Thank you," Ishbel said. And this time she was allowed to ascend the stairs by herself.

Lawyer Timothy Slade was resting in his favorite chair, his gout-ridden foot stretched out on a footstool. He gestured to Ishbel with his ebony cane, indicating that she take a chair near him.

He said, "I haven't seen you for a little while."

"No, I intended to come by, but so many things have happened."

"I gathered that," the old man said dryly. "I saw the police officer visit your house this morning—at least, one of my servants did, and the word was passed on to me."

She smiled ruefully. "Mrs. Needles was afraid of that. She's sure our reputation in the square will suffer."

Lawyer Slade said, "I'm concerned about why you called in the police."

"I was attacked in the garden last night. Someone came up behind me and tried to throttle me. I was rescued by Chen, who heard my scream, and Simpson, who arrived on the scene shortly afterwards."

The old man looked astounded. "You were attacked!"

"Yes. There were indications that someone may have come over the wall."

"So you think it was a burglar?"

"Henry seems sure that it was an intruder of some sort."

"And the police?"

"They're investigating it. They aren't sure."

Lawyer Slade raised his eyebrows. "Not sure, eh? Then they feel it could have been someone within the household?"

"There is that possibility."

"Was Henry at home?"

"Yes."

"He didn't hear your scream?" The lawyer's tone indicated more than his words. She had the strong feeling that he was offering an indirect accusation of her husband.

She said, "He was in the study."

"As he so often is!" Again there was irony in the old man's tone.

"True," she said. "The door was closed. He wasn't able to hear me. I only managed to scream once."

"This is too bad," the old lawyer said with a dismal expression on his wizened face.

"I know," she said. "I feel safer in the house now that I have Simpson."

"The fishmonger fellow you hired to replace Griffin?"

"Yes. He is extremely loyal to me."

"I'm glad to hear it," Lawyer Slade said. He sat forward in his chair rather tensely, his hands balanced on the knob of his cane. "I have something bizarre to tell you. In fact, you may find it hard to believe."

So there was to be another revelation. Ishbel sat up very straight and prepared herself for whatever she was about to hear. In a small voice she said, "Tell me."

The ancient face of the lawyer took on an awed look. He said, "I saw a ghost the other night. The first I have ever seen in my life."

"Oh?"

He nodded solemnly. "I saw the ghost of Patricia!"

"Patricia!" she echoed him, for she had somehow guessed that was what he might say.

"I was hobbling by the front windows late in the evening," he went on. "I saw a figure standing in the center of the square. I thought she looked familiar. She was staring at Number Twenty-Two as if hesitating before going in there. Then she gazed at the other houses and I caught a glimpse of her face. Even at a distance and in the moonlight I was able to identify the face as belonging to Patricia!"

"Then what?"

"I tried to quickly make my way downstairs and out," he said. "I should not have attempted it. But somehow I managed, though it took me a long while. By the time I reached the front door and flung it open to call to her, there was no longer any sign of her. She had vanished."

Ishbel said, "I'm not quite as surprised as you might expect. For I have also seen the same phantom."

"You have?"

"Yes."

"Did you tell your husband?"

"I did. He refused to take me seriously. He said I had imagined it!"

"That is very strange," the old lawyer said. "Until now I have never accepted that there are such things as ghosts. I'm no longer so sure."

"I know how you feel. But I wonder if our ghost isn't of more substance than we suspect. I wonder if we aren't dealing with a living person."

"Patricia is dead!" he gasped.

"We have assumed so," she said. "But can we be sure? You were one of the first called in. Did you ascertain for yourself that she was dead?"

"No. Henry informed me that she was."

"What about a doctor?"

"I called Dr. Smith," the lawyer said, "but only to have him sign that she was legally dead. By that time Lord Carney had come and taken Patricia's body with him."

"What if there was still a breath of life in her that Henry didn't even suspect? Suppose her father discovered this and had her nursed back to health?"

The old man stared at her in shocked silence for a moment. "I don't know what to say. It might have happened, but I don't think it did."

"By all accounts no one saw her buried; no one has visited her grave."

"Lord Carney is old and was badly shattered by the tragedy. No one wished to bother him further."

"Some mystery woman has paid Henry visits at night. I

have smelled opium in the room after she has left. He has always denied the existence of such a person. But it has been these visits that have changed him from a normal, kindly husband to an aloof, frightened one. Can it be that Patricia is returning to taunt him?"

"You actually think that?"

"I think she may have become a drug addict and all the bizarre events that have happened may be a direct result of that."

Lawyer Slade stared at her. "But if Patricia is still alive, your position and that of your children is untenable!"

"I know," she agreed. "Henry is a bigamist, though probably an innocent one."

"It all hinges on whether Patricia was really dead or not," the lawyer said. "And I must say, I believe that she was."

"Yet you have seen her and so have I! How do you explain that?"

"I can't explain it," he admitted. "Perhaps Henry is right. Perhaps we are both in error. This could be some woman who resembles Patricia."

"To such a degree? And to turn up here mysteriously? I'd say the chances are all against it."

"What do you propose to do about it?"

"The police detective seemed very competent," she said. "I hope that he will keep digging at the mystery until he comes up with something. If Patricia is still alive, she is bound to be seen by others. Sooner or later she will be found out."

"It is very confusing," Lawyer Slade sighed.

"I know. I even spoke to Peter Graves about seeing a phantom Patricia, and he disputed the possibility. He became quite angry about it."

"He was in love with her."

"I realize that," she said. "And yet there were many things he did not know about her. He clung to an idealized image that was never quite the true Patricia."

"What action can you take personally to protect yourself?"

"I will be more cautious about going into the garden alone at night. And when I can, I'm going to have Simpson drive me out to Lord Carney's estate. I want to talk to that old man and ask him to show me where Patricia is buried."

"He has become a recluse. He may not see you," Lawyer Slade warned.

"I think he would if I came with an introduction from you," she said. "You are old friends."

The wizened face of the white-haired man showed a slight frown. "You want me to write a note requesting that he see you?"

"If you will. It is a way you can help."

He did not hesitate. He said, "There is a quill pen, ink, and paper on the desk over there. Bring them to me."

She did as he requested and stood by while he wrote the short note and signed it with a flourish. When the ink was dry, he placed the message in an envelope and addressed it to Lord Carney. Then he handed it to her.

She said, "Thank you. I will let you know what happens."

"I want your word on that," the old lawyer said. "It is a frustration to sit here a cripple and have everything happening beyond my reach."

"Never fear," she said with a small smile. "I will make a point of keeping you informed from now on."

"When will you go to see Lord Carney?"

"Tomorrow, if all is well," she said. "I do not know what the police may find out in the meantime."

The old lawyer nodded. Then he gave her a word of warning. "I do not think you should trust Peter Graves too far. He is Henry's avowed enemy. I realize I sent you to him, but it was never my intention that you two should become close friends. I wanted you to get whatever information you could from him without giving him much in return."

On her feet to go, she said, "I have tried to do that. But I must confess I find him more likable than I expected."

"He has charm," the old man grudgingly agreed. "I'm not sure that he puts it to the best advantage."

"Many of us fail in that regard," she said. "Now I will be on my way. Think over what I have told you."

"I will think of little else," he grumbled. "I now see my stupidity in not making sure myself that Patricia was dead. I failed my duty in that."

"It was a nasty business. The tragedy shook your judgment."

"That is a kind way of putting it," Lawyer Slade said. "But I fear it was more the bumbling incompetence of an old man used as an unknowing accomplice by your husband. That is, if what you have suggested should turn out to be true."

"Don't condemn yourself needlessly," Ishbel said. "It may turn out that I am completely wrong."

She left the old man with this small comfort and went on to do her shopping. It was not too surprising that she was unable to put her mind on her purchases. She wound up accomplishing very little. The store clerks were polite, and the man in the drygoods shop filled the counter with displays of bolts of cloth.

"I'm unable to make a selection today," she finally told him as she slipped down from the tall stool facing the counter.

The polite young man with hair parted in the middle smiled wanly. "That is quite all right, madam. Though I have shown you everything in sateen that I have available."

"Some of the colors are excellent," she said. "I'll come back another day when I'm feeling better."

"By all means, madam," the clerk said. And then, as an afterthought, "Would you care to see our latest shipment of silks?"

"No. It would be a waste of your time, and I've taken quite enough of it already."

She made her way out of the shop feeling guilty but knowing that her mind was too filled with other thoughts to allow her to concentrate on material for her new gown. She made her way back to Number Twenty-Two, grateful for the protection of the parasol; the sun was now high in the sky and strong.

The information Lawyer Slade had given her had persuaded her that she must be right in thinking Patricia alive. She now had the letter of introduction from the old lawyer as a first step in her project of interviewing Lord Carney. She was so absorbed with these thoughts that she failed to see the door of Number Twenty-Eight open as she came by it. Then a well-dressed Peter Graves appeared and came down the steps.

He doffed his top hat and smiled at her. "This is a more suitable time to be on the streets than when I met you last."

She held her parasol back so she might get a good look at him. She said, "I realize now your advice was good. I shall be more cautious in the future."

He glanced towards Number Twenty-Two and in a mocking fashion asked, "How are you managing with the phantoms?"

"I'm trying to forget about them."

"You won't find it easy. Patricia didn't. She told me the house always gave her a feeling of terror. She sensed some hidden menace in it, poor girl."

Changing the subject because she found it awkward, Ishbel asked, "Is your cousin Doris still in London?"

"No. She has returned home. I miss her."

"She seemed very nice. Did you get to the Duke of Clarendon's party?"

"It was a delightful affair," Peter Graves assured her. "Has Henry taken you to the theater again?"

"I'm afraid not."

"What a pity! There's a new comedy that is excellent. Makes fun of one of the late Prince Regent's lady friends. You would enjoy it."

"It sounds amusing," she said. "I must tell Henry about it."

The dandified artist smiled grimly. "I doubt if he'll show any interest. Patricia found him a dullard, devoted only to his precious tea business."

"One has to give time to one's work," she offered. "What about your painting?"

"I have a number of commissions," he said airily. "At the moment I'm on my way to have sherry with the Dowager Lady Buick. I'm to do her portrait."

"Good luck," she said.

"And the same to you," Peter Graves said with a smirk. Then he returned his top hat to his head and got in the waiting carriage to be driven off.

Ishbel continued on her way to Number Twenty-Two. She found the artist something of an enigma. She felt there was a good deal more to him than he allowed others to know. Yet he was frank enough about his hatred of her husband and his admiration for the late Patricia—if she was the "late" Patricia.

Surely, Ishbel thought, if Patricia were alive the artist would know it. He had been as close to her as anyone. On the other hand, if Patricia had not told him the name of her lover, there must have been many other things she hadn't told him. So there was a small chance that Henry Davis's first wife could be alive without Peter Graves' being aware of it.

When Ishbel reached Number Twenty-Two, Mrs. Needles let her in and in a low voice informed her, "Someone here to see you."

"Who is it?"

Mrs. Needles looked worried. "A girl who used to work here. She marched up to the door as bold as brass and asked to speak to you."

"Oh?"

The old woman's wrinkled face remained shadowed with concern. "I daresay I'm taking a terrible risk. If the master were here, he'd be that angry with me. He didn't like this girl. He dismissed her right after Mrs. Patricia fell down the stairs to her death."

"What did the girl do?"

"She was a personal maid to Mrs. Patricia," the old woman said. "Had a right fit of hysterics when Mrs. Patricia met her death. It was then the master dismissed her."

"I see," she said. "What is her name?"

"Clara Sawyer. She puts on the airs of a lady, but she is no more than a lady's maid. Just now she claims to be working for the wife of Lambert, the wine merchant."

"Have you any idea why she wants to see me?"

"No. She wouldn't tell me," Mrs. Needles said. "I was going to send her on her way, and then I decided I'd better not."

"I'm glad you didn't," Ishbel said, giving the housekeeper the parasol and the package with the ribbons she'd bought for her bonnet. "Where is she?"

"In the back parlor," Mrs. Needles said with a look of condescension. "I wasn't going to put the likes of her in the living room."

"Thank you, Mrs. Needles," she said. "I'll go see her at once."

She went down the hall to the door of the back parlor. Inside, a short young woman in a brown dress and a light straw bonnet stood gazing out the window at the garden. When Ishbel entered the room, the girl turned around quickly. She had yellowish hair and a V-shaped pale face with a hint of buck teeth, which prevented her from being pretty. Her eyes were fairly large and dark blue, and now they were fixed on Ishbel in an almost frightened fashion.

Ishbel went in to her and held out her hand. "I'm Mrs. Davis. I understand that your name is Clara Sawyer and that you were the personal maid to my husband's first wife."

Clara Sawyer shook hands with her nervously and in a taut, high-pitched voice said, "I suppose Mrs. Needles told you all that—and no doubt a lot of other things not too nice about me!"

"There was no long discussion of you. I am surprised that you wish to see me."

The girl was very tense. "I've come to warn you, ma'am."

"Warn me? About what?"

The girl hesitated and then pointed to the door. "May I please shut the door? I don't want what I'm about to say to be overheard."

"All right," Ishbel said, puzzled by the girl's odd behavior.

Clara went over and shut the door, then returned to her. "What I have to say is for your ears alone."

"Go on," Ishbel urged her.

The blond girl's manner was frightened. "I'm taking a chance even coming here."

"Are you?"

"Yes. If Mr. Davis was here he'd not let me in. And he'd see that I got punished for my impudence."

"Please explain your visit."

The girl's eyes met hers. "Someone tried to murder you last night."

"How do you know that?"

"All the help here are friends of mine. One of them let me know what went on in the garden last night."

"Who told you?"

"I can't give you the name yet," Clara Sawyer said. "I may later when I know you better."

"Please continue."

"When I was Mrs. Patricia's personal maid, she trusted me. She was good to me. There's not anything I wouldn't do for her."

"And?"

"I was here the night she died in that fall. And when I heard what happened to you, I had to come and warn you."

"You were here the night of Patricia's death?"

"Yes, ma'am, and I don't believe she fell accidentally. I say that she was shoved down those stairs by someone who ought to have loved her."

"Really?" Ishbel was trying hard not to betray any emotion.

"I don't want it to happen to you . . . because he is mad!"

"Who is mad!"

"The master!" the tiny girl said emotionally. "It's the opium. He tried to call her a drug addict, and I'm sure it was him all along!"

"What makes you so sure?"

"Things I heard and things I saw," the girl declared. "They were always fighting! She would burst out of the study in tears!"

"You are making a very serious allegation," she warned the girl.

"I don't care," Clara cried. "First that old Miss Betsy Davis, who brought Mr. Henry up, came here and was cruel to my mistress. And when she left, it was the master."

"Why were they cruel to Patricia?"

The girl looked sullen. "The master was always accusing her of seeing Mr. Graves and of having other lovers."

"Wasn't that true?"

Clara hesitated. "If it was, he drove her to it with his drug taking!"

"Then you do know it to be true? That she was seeing other men?"

"She did it because she was so unhappy here," Clara said in a low voice. "She told me so."

"Then my husband and Miss Betsy Davis were right in what they said about her."

"It wasn't her fault, and he killed her because of it," the girl said. "And because he's mad he'll kill you also."

"Is that what you came here to tell me?"

"Yes."

"These are serious things you're saying. I could turn you over to the police and have them make you prove your allegations."

"No, ma'am!" The girl sounded frightened. "Don't bring the police into it. They'll side with him, and he'll make sure something awful will happen to me!"

"You sound frightened of my husband."

"I am," the girl said, "and so was Mrs. Patricia. I have a letter here that proves it."

"Will you let me see it?"

"You can read it," Clara told her. "If I let you keep it, I must be paid. I must have something for the risk I'm taking!"

So it was money, not loyalty to her dead mistress, that had brought the girl here, Ishbel decided. She said, "If I think the letter is important enough I will pay you."

Uneasily the girl brought out a folded sheet of paper from her pocket. "I found this on the floor of the bedroom the night Mrs. Patricia met her death."

Ishbel was trembling a little as she took the note and opened it. The paper was badly crinkled, as if someone had decided to dispose of it and had crushed it into a ball, but the writing on it was still legible. She read, "Dear L, I am in danger. He has threatened me. Perhaps you can somehow manage to keep him in hand!, Patricia." She read the letter twice and then asked the girl, "Do you know who 'L' is?"

"No."

"You're sure?"

"She didn't tell me. I only knew about certain of her friends," the girl declared nervously. "But she meant to send that message and then changed her mind. I found it crushed in a ball on the floor after she was shoved down the stairs."

"You assume this letter means she was afraid of her husband?"

"Who else?"

"It doesn't mention him by name."

"It had to be him," Clara Sawyer insisted. "He had been quarreling with her about her lover."

Ishbel sighed and studied the letter again. Then she lifted it to her nose and found a faint odor of perfume still on it. Violets! It clearly had been written by Patricia.

She asked the girl, "What do you want for it?"

"Five pounds."

"I'll give it to you. What else can you tell me?"

"I know the address of the man she was seeing and his name," the girl said.

Ishbel felt her heart pound more fiercely. In a voice she tried hard to control, she asked, "Are you willing to sell me that information?"

"Yes."

"How much?"

"Ten pounds," the girl said.

"I'll pay you."

"I'd like my five pounds first," Clara told her.

"One moment," she said. "I'll get it." And she left the girl alone in the room while she hurried up the shadowed stairs and found her purse in the dresser drawer. She had taken only a limited amount of money to the shops with her, and it had not been nearly five pounds. But she had the fifteen pounds required in her room, in the purse that was hidden under clothes in the dresser drawer.

Armed with the money, she started back down the stairs. She felt like a sleepwalker in the midst of a dread nightmare, a nightmare from which she couldn't escape. She knew that what Clara Sawyer was doing was wrong and not in her interest, yet she felt obliged to find out all she could about Patricia, and the girl seemed to have a store of information.

Entering the room again she closed the door and gave Clara the promised five pounds. The girl took the notes greedily and stuffed them in her bosom.

Ishbel said, "Now, about the name and address of the man Mrs. Patricia was seeing. . . ."

The girl hesitated, "I can't give it to you now."

"I have the ten pounds," she said, showing the money to her.

"I can't tell you until later. I don't know the name and address by memory. I have it on a slip of paper in my room."

"When can you bring the information to me?"

"Tomorrow night would be my first chance," Clara said.

"I shall have the money waiting for you."

"I daren't risk Mr. Henry seeing me," the girl said in frightened protest.

"You needn't be seen," Ishbel told her. "Come to the side door, and I'll arrange for Mrs. Needles to leave it unlocked."

"Where will you be?"

"In this room," Ishbel said. "You can come directly in here. I'll be waiting with the money."

"And you won't tell the mister?"

"Depend on that."

"He'd be liable to do both of us in," the girl warned her solemnly.

"I'll see your visit is kept secret," she promised.

"But won't the mister be in the house?"

"He's always in his study in the evenings," she said.

Clara gave a deep sigh. "All right, then. I'll be here to-morrow night at eight sharp."

"Come straight here to this room," Ishbel said. "And I hope you can vouch for your information's being accurate."

"It is," the girl assured her. "I'll give you his name and where he lives."

Ishbel gave her a stern look. "You know what you are doing is unlawful?"

"I'm only trying to help you," the blond girl whined.

"I hope that is true," Ishbel said. "I will protect you if the name and address prove to be the true ones. If the information is incorrect, I will turn you over to the police."

"Don't do that, ma'am!" the girl pleaded.

"I won't if you prove to be truthful," Ishbel said. "But if you lie to me or if you don't return tomorrow night, I will call on the detective who was here this morning and tell him all about you."

"You won't have to, ma'am," Clara said. "I'll be back!"

Chapter Eight

After Clara Sawyer left, Ishbel sought out Mrs. Needles and told her that the girl would be returning. She said, "I have her promise she will come back tomorrow night and bring some important information with her."

"I don't trust her," the old woman grumbled. "I never have."

"Still, I must find out if she is telling the truth or not," Ishbel said as she stood with the housekeeper in the back hallway.

"I'll let her in, but if the master finds out, it will be bad for both of us," the housekeeper warned.

"I will take the responsibility," Ishbel said.

She then went upstairs and carefully hid away the letter addressed to "L." She had no idea who this unknown "L" might be, but apparently it was someone Patricia had trusted and who knew about her affair and her constant quarrels with Henry. Perhaps "L" stood simply for "Love" or "Lover." The note seemed to offer damning evidence against Henry; if it were to be taken literally, it indicated that Patricia had feared for her life. And only a few hours after writing it, she was found dead at the bottom of the stairs.

But what if it should turn out that Patricia wasn't dead after all? This was the question to which Ishbel felt she must find the answer. She had the old lawyer's letter of introduction to Lord Carney, and as soon as possible she intended to go and question the old man about his daughter.

She had barely hidden away the letter sold her by Clara when she heard a familiar footstep in the hall outside. It was early in the afternoon for Henry to return home, but she was sure it was his step. This was confirmed a moment later when he appeared in the doorway.

She said, "You're home very early."

"I have to take the stage to Liverpool this evening," he said. "Company business. I came home to pack."

"How long will you be gone?"

"It depends," he said, going to the closet for his valise. "I'll be away tonight and tomorrow at least, and likely tomorrow night as well. I'll make an effort to be back on the morning stage the following day."

Ishbel was both bothered and pleased. She disliked being left alone in the old house for several nights, but she was pleased that Henry would be out of London since his absence would give her freedom to make the enquiries she wished.

She said, "I don't like being here by myself."

He set the valise on the bed and opened it in preparation for packing. "You won't be alone. Mrs. Needles and all the servants are here."

"That's not the same as having one's husband close by."

"There's nothing for you to fear," he said in his cool fashion, as he crossed between valise and dresser, starting to pack.

"The detective came this morning."

"I know," he said, as he kept busy. "I stopped at the police station and gave them all the details."

"His name was Detective Hawker and he seemed to think I had cause to fear."

"Indeed," her husband said. "What sort of theory did he come up with?"

"He had an idea my attacker might not have been an intruder."

Henry glanced up from packing the valise and frowned.

"That's nonsense," he said. "He saw the fence, didn't he? It indicated clearly that someone had climbed over it."

"Detective Hawker thought that might have been staged to divert attention from the real criminal. He thought it possible I was attacked by someone within the house."

"Someone within the house!" her handsome husband echoed in annoyance. "Then I say the man is a fool."

"You never did hope for much help from the police," she reminded him.

"I didn't, and it seems I was right," he replied. He closed the valise and lifted it from the bed in his right hand. Then he came over to her and gave her a perfunctory kiss. He said, "Just be careful until I return. No walking in the garden at night by yourself. Nothing like that."

"I'll remember," she said quietly. "I wish I could go with you."

"Completely out of the question," her husband said. "Now I can't tarry any longer or I'll miss my stage." And he marched out of the room. A moment later she heard him descending the stairs.

She stood at the bedroom window and watched him get quickly into a waiting carriage and be driven off. As she watched the carriage vanish around the corner of the street, she had the uneasy feeling that her husband had lied to her. She thought that he wasn't leaving the city at all but rather was probably having a secret rendezvous somewhere with the mystery woman. Was it possible that Patricia was alive and he was meeting her?

She at once sat down and composed an urgent note to her cousin Ernest. In the note she begged him to come and see her at the earliest moment. She gave the note to Mrs. Needles with the request that a maid be sent with it to the address Ernest had given her as his lodging place.

With that out of the way, she summoned Simpson and asked him, "Simpson, would you mind driving me to an estate on the other side of London?"

"Not at all, ma'am," the big man said. "Where do you wish to be driven?"

"To Lord Carney's estate," she said. "It's not too far outside London."

The big man nodded. "Indeed, I know where it is. I've had it pointed out to me. Regular castle there, ma'am."

"I wish to be driven there directly after dinner," she said. "Will you have the carriage ready?"

"That I will, ma'am," the burly man with the black eye patch promised.

Dinner was a tense, lonely experience for her, and she ate very little. She left the table at the earliest possible moment and went upstairs to change into a modest brown traveling suit with a bonnet of the same shade. Then she came down to find Chen standing by the open front door.

The old Chinese said, "The carriage is waiting, missee."

She told Chen, "If my cousin or anyone else calls, let them know I'll be back as early as possible."

"Yes, missee," Chen said with a nod.

Simpson was waiting to help her into the carriage. He told her in a quick aside, "The Chinese gent wanted to know where I was taking you."

"Did you tell him?"

Simpson smiled wisely. "Not me, ma'am. I know when to keep my mouth shut."

"I'm glad that you do, Simpson," she said, as he closed the carriage door and took his seat up front.

He managed the single horse nicely. By skirting the main streets, they crossed the city more quickly than she had hoped. And it seemed a very short while until she was being driven up a driveway lined with giant elms. At the end of the drive there was an elegant country house.

Simpson helped her to the ground, and she ordered him to wait for her. Then she presented herself at the imposing front entrance of the mansion. When the door was opened by a venerable butler, she handed him the envelope given her by the old lawyer.

The butler studied the envelope and told her, "Do come in, Mrs. Davis. I will speak to the master and see if he will talk to you. He has been unwell of late."

She braved a smile. "Tell him I promise not to keep him long."

The butler said, "They all promise him that, but few keep their word."

"I'm a little early," she said, "but I wanted to catch him before he retired."

"That was wise, ma'am," the butler said. "Lord Carney goes to bed very early since his second round of illness this spring."

"I had not heard about it."

"Very serious," the grave-faced butler informed her. "If you will make yourself comfortable, I will take your message to him."

"Thank you," she said and sat on an ornate chair in the great reception hall. It was tremendously high of ceiling and made the reception hall at Castle Square seem tiny by comparison. A great cut-glass chandelier hung from the ceiling, and several huge, colorful paintings adorned the walls.

The big house was weirdly quiet, as if there was no one living in it. She supposed that Lord Carney was living alone now that Patricia was dead. Presumably his wife had died earlier and they only had the one child.

After what seemed an age she heard the slow footsteps of
the butler as he came down the winding, gray stairway. He
crossed over to her and said, "Lord Carney will receive you in
his bedroom. He has already retired for the night."

"I'm sorry to bother him," she said, rising.

"It does not matter," the butler said. "He is awake. It is his
habit to read from the Bible at this hour."

"Oh?" she said, recalling Lawyer Timothy Slade's remark
that the old Lord had been a rake in his day and in his old age
had turned to religion in a fanatical way.

"If you will come with me," the butler said.

Ascending the stairway, she asked him, "Does Lord
Carney live here alone?"

"His lordship has no one left at all," the butler said sadly.
"He is the last of his line."

"Tragic," she agreed politely.

"Had Miss Patricia lived and borne children, it would
have been another story," the butler said.

"True."

When they reached the landing, the butler marched ahead
along a broad, richly decorated corridor and suddenly halted by
an open door. He gestured. "His lordship is in there, ma'am."

"Thank you," she said and rather timorously entered the
huge bedroom, which was filled with the odor of oil of pep-
permint. At first she thought the bed was empty, but as she
drew nearer to it, she saw the cadaverous, pale face the same
shade as the pillow and the domed bald head of the ancient
Lord Carney.

He had a Bible in his hands and he studied her over it. In a
surprisingly loud, booming voice he said, "So you are the
woman that Henry chose to replace my daughter!"

"Yes," she said nervously. "Lawyer Slade was kind
enough to give me the letter of introduction to you."

"What is it you want?" Lord Carney asked brusquely. "You have interrupted my Bible reading."

"Forgive me," she said. "I have come to ask you about your daughter."

"About my daughter?"

"I'm concerned about the way she met her death," Ishbel said. "There seems to be a great deal of mystery about it."

Lord Carney glared at her like a pale old eagle. He demanded, "Why should you come here questioning me about Patricia's death?"

"As Henry Davis's second wife I would like to know the truth of what happened."

The old man was taken with a sudden bout of coughing. When he recovered from it, he waved a frail hand at her and told her, "My daughter is dead. There is an old saying 'Let the dead rest.' I suggest you heed it."

Ishbel said, "Are you satisfied her death was truly an accident?"

A strange expression crossed the pale, cadaverous face. He said, "I lost my daughter. It was the Lord's will! I am not one to question His doings."

Ishbel was certain that for some reason he was carefully evading her questioning. He was putting her off with vague replies. She tried another tack. "Why did you bring her here for burial?"

"I wanted her last resting place to be the family vault," the old man said in his booming voice. "I did not want her buried among strangers."

"Wives are usually buried with their husbands," she countered.

"You are Henry's wife now," was his reply. "I am weary and I do not wish to be bothered with such questions. If you have nothing more to say, I suggest you be on your way."

"I regret disturbing you," she said. "May I ask one more favor of you?"

"What?"

"May I see Patricia's casket in the vault? Would you have someone take me to look at it?"

"No." The reply was emphatic.

"Why not?"

"Because it is none of your business, young woman," the old man boomed angrily. "I have no more time for you. I bid you good evening!"

"Very well," she said quietly. "I only wish you had felt you could be frank with me."

"I have nothing more to say," Lord Carney told her. He picked up the Bible and began reading it once more.

Ishbel was depressed by the cold reception the old man had given her. Yet she was of the opinion her time hadn't been entirely wasted. He had shown a fear of her finding out too much about his daughter's death, and he had refused to allow her to see her burial place. Both evasions caused her to suspect that it was possible Patricia was not dead, that she had recovered under care in her father's mansion and was now pursuing some vengeful plan of her own.

If Henry had actually attempted to shove her down the steps to her death, it was possible that Patricia might be ready to make him pay dearly for what he had done. And surely one of Patricia's targets would be the second wife who had replaced her. Ishbel gave a tiny shudder as she descended the broad stairway and prepared to leave the great, silent house. There was nothing more to be learned there for the moment.

Simpson was waiting in the driveway with the carriage. As the big man with black eye patch helped her into the vehicle, he asked, "Was your journey a profitable one, ma'am?"

She shook her head. "I'm afraid not. I learned very little here."

He studied her earnestly. "Is it the master you are afraid of, ma'am?"

Startled, she asked, "What made you say that?"

"There are whisperings in the house that all is not well between you two," the big man said.

"You mustn't listen to such talk," she told him. "Take me back to Castle Square as quickly as you can."

"Yes, ma'am," Simpson said and closed the carriage door.

All during the drive back to Number Twenty-Two she sat back and tried to make some pattern of the various threads she was familiar with. Patricia had been unfaithful to Henry with some mysterious lover. There had been quarrels between the two, ending with the accident on the stairs that had supposedly taken Patricia's life. Then Lord Carney had suddenly appeared on the scene and had taken the body of his daughter away with him.

There were no proper death certificates or burial records, and Lord Carney had refused to let Ishbel enter the vault where Patricia was supposedly buried. It all made Ishbel suspicious that Patricia was still alive. She had seen the phantom figure with Patricia's face that foggy night, and old Lawyer Slade had reported seeing a ghostly Patricia. It had to mean either that Patricia's ghost was returning to haunt the house at Castle Square or that Patricia herself was alive and coming back to torment Henry in some way, perhaps to blackmail him for opium if she were a crazed drug addict. Either way it was a terrifying business.

By the time the carriage arrived back at Castle Square, it was dark. As Ishbel gazed out the windows of the vehicle she saw that there was a light showing from an upstairs window of Lawyer Slade's house at Twenty-Six and lights in the downstairs windows of artist Peter Graves' house at Number Twenty-Eight. The windows of Number Twenty-Two showed no lights at all.

Simpson helped her down from the carriage, and she went up to the door of Twenty-Two. A few minutes later Mrs. Needles appeared to open it for her. "You are late returning, ma'am," the old woman said. "I was beginning to worry about you."

"We had rather a long journey," she said. "Is there any news?"

The old woman nodded. "Yes. The maid delivered your message to your cousin. And he sent back word by her that he would be here tomorrow morning."

"Good," she said, encouraged by the news.

"Would you care for something to eat or drink before you retire?" the housekeeper asked.

"No," she said. "I'm tired. I think I will go straight up to bed."

She mounted the dark stairway, and as she reached the landing the elderly Chen came gliding out from the shadows. He stood by for her to pass him before he continued down the stairs.

She asked him, "What are you doing up here?"

"A window was open and a shutter was clattering, missee," the old Chinese said.

She knew he had no duties that took him upstairs at night and felt his excuse for being there was a shallow one. It would be much more likely that he'd been rummaging through the bedroom she and Henry occupied. At once she began to worry about whether she had been careful enough in hiding that letter she had purchased from Clara Sawyer. Perhaps Chen had been after that.

But she said nothing. She hurried on to the bedroom. As

soon as she was safely inside, she went to the dresser drawer where she had hidden the letter under the paper covering at the bottom of the drawer. The candle on the dresser offered only a weak glow of light by which to make her frenzied search. She was more frightened than surprised to discover that this letter had vanished in the same way as the other one! It had to be Chen!

Thinking she might have made a mistake as to which drawer she'd hidden the letter in, she began making a frantic check of the bottom drawer. It was while she was doing this that her hand came into contact with a small, cold, metal object. She pushed back the clothes that concealed it and found herself staring down at a tiny pistol!

She gazed at it with fascinated eyes and then with some timidity lifted it out to examine it. Though it was a small weapon, it appeared to be lethal enough, and by the weight of it she judged it to be loaded. Her dismay turned to partial relief as she realized that by pure chance she had come upon a weapon to defend herself with.

She had no idea how it might have gotten there. Had Patricia secreted it away when she feared for her life? If so, Ishbel had somehow not noticed it when placing her own things in the dresser. But perhaps that was natural. The bottom drawer had contained extra blankets, and the pistol had been tucked away under these blankets.

After she prepared for bed, she placed the pistol under her pillow where it would be fairly easy to reach. Then she slipped between the sheets and extinguished the candle on her dresser. She stared up into the darkness and wondered where Henry might be. Had her husband really gone to Liverpool or was he somewhere in London? This worried her.

She was also concerned about whether or not Patricia was alive and what part she was playing in all this. Her troubled thoughts kept her from sleep. The space beside her in the wide bed reminded her that she was alone. After a while sheer exhaustion took over, and her eyes closed in sleep.

With sleep came a series of tormented dreams. She was back at Lord Carney's estate, and against the wishes of the old peer she was entering the family cemetery behind the gray stone mansion. It was a moonlit night, and the gravestones pointed weirdly to the sky like threatening black fingers. Trembling, she made her way between them until she came to the enormous family vault with CARNEY in huge letters above its iron door.

Fearfully she opened the rusty door and stepped into the vault. The moonlight followed her through the open door so that she was able to make out the shelves on either side of the dank interior. Cobwebbed and dust-covered caskets were stacked one above the other. She timidly approached the casket nearest her to attempt to see whether there was a marking plate on it or not. She fought back her fright and wiped away the cobwebs and dust with her hand.

She was leaning closer to see if there was a name plate on the casket when she heard the sound from deep within the vault. It was a low, moaning sound, and as she quickly glanced into the shadows ahead of her, she saw a familiar figure! It was Patricia, garbed all in white, her eyes wide and staring, a strange, bewildered expression on her lovely face. With hands outstretched the weird vision came closer to her!

Ishbel let out a scream and came awake. But she awakened to her nightmare! At the side of her bed and advancing on her was the ghostly figure of Patricia, in white and looking the same dazed way she had in the dream! Almost automatically Ishbel reached for the tiny pistol under her pillow. She drew it out and fired point blank at the phantom figure. The tiny weapon emitted a loud blast and blaze. And at the same instant Ishbel fainted.

When she opened her eyes, Mrs. Needles was standing by her bedside holding a candle. The wrinkled face of the housekeeper showed alarm. "What ever made you fire that pistol, ma'am?"

Ishbel sat up and saw the gun on the counterpane where it had dropped from her hand. Memory of what had happened flooded back to her. She said, "There was a ghost in the room! I fired at it!"

"A ghost?" the old woman echoed.

"Patricia's ghost! All in white! She came into the room and was coming towards me!"

"You must have had a bad dream!" the housekeeper quavered.

"No," Ishbel said. "She did come into the room. I found the pistol, and I aimed at her and fired."

The old woman held the candle higher and gazed around her. "There's no one in the room. You could not have shot anyone!"

Ishbel asked, "No blood on the floor?"

Mrs. Needles lowered the candle and gazed at the floor. "None!"

Ishbel said grimly, "Probably ghosts don't bleed."

The old woman seemed badly shocked. She said, "I heard the shot and came at once. What will the master say?"

"I don't care much what he says," was Ishbel's reply. "I had to defend myself. I'm only disgusted that I fainted at the most important moment."

"What shall I do?" Mrs. Needles wanted to know.

"There's nothing to be done," Ishbel said. "We'll simply have to wait and see what another day brings."

"Will you be all right alone in here?"

"Yes. Leave me a lighted candle. And I'll keep this pistol handy. I doubt very much whether the ghost will bother me again."

As it turned out, her prediction was right. Nothing came to worry her for the rest of the night. In the morning she carefully hid the pistol beneath the blankets in the lower drawer again. She was convinced something dreadful would have happened to her if she had not had the weapon.

Shortly after breakfast she had a visitor. It was the squat, bow-legged Detective Hawker. She received him in the living room, and he apologized for bothering her.

He said, "I have come here with a warning."

"Oh?"

The stout detective was solemn. "You have a former criminal here in your employ. Did you know that?"

"No," she said. "Who is it?"

"Your new man Simpson," Detective Hawker said. "I had an idea I'd seen him before, and I didn't think it was merely as a fishmonger in the streets. I saw him in the law courts when he was sentenced to a year in prison for violently assaulting a man."

"Are you sure?"

"Positive. The man he assaulted was a suspected thief. He and Simpson were cronies, so it would follow that he also has been a thief."

"I'm surprised," she said. "He has been a good worker here and has given me no trouble."

"Probably because as soon as he knows all the secrets of the house, he will rob you and vanish. That is what I'd expect from him."

"I believe you're wrong. I'm of the opinion he has reformed and is trying to live a better life."

Detective Hawker shrugged. "So far we have nothing on

him. If you want to speak for him, it is your privilege. I'm willing to let him stay on here and see if he leads us to anything."

"You definitely think he is here for no good?" she said unhappily.

"I do. It was likely he who attacked you in the garden. Later we may be able to prove that. Where is your husband?"

"In Liverpool. He left yesterday."

"Liverpool?" the old man said with a strange look. "That is too bad. I had a few questions for him. Well, they can wait."

"What sort of questions?"

"I'd rather wait to announce them," the stout Detective Hawker said. "Do you know if he and Simpson ever had any dealings before Simpson came here?"

"I can't imagine that they did. I was the one who spoke of hiring Simpson. My husband wasn't enthusiastic about the idea."

"Or maybe pretended he wasn't," Detective Hawker said shrewdly.

She gazed up at him with alarm. "You think they may be in league?"

"It's a possibility. At this moment anything is a possibility. Have you anything new to tell me?"

"Yes," she said. "A girl came here and sold me a letter Patricia had written. The girl was formerly Patricia's personal maid, and Henry dismissed her after the accident."

"May I see the letter?"

Her cheeks crimsoned. "I'm afraid not. I hid it away and it somehow vanished."

Detective Hawker looked bleak. "That's unfortunate," he said dryly. "You ought to have called me at once."

"I behaved stupidly," she admitted.

"What did the letter say? Do you remember?"

"Yes. It was addressed to someone named 'L'."

" 'L'? Do you have any idea who it might be?"

"No, not at the moment," she said. "In the letter Patricia said she was terrified. That she was sure an attempt was going to be made on her life."

"When was this letter written?"

"The maid says on the night of her death."

Detective Hawker frowned. "Doesn't sound too good for your husband."

"I know," she agreed.

"I want to talk with this maid," Detective Hawker said. "Do you know where I can find her?"

"No," she said. "But she has promised to return with the name and address of Patricia's lover. I expect to receive that information from her tonight. I don't think you should bother her until after I buy the information from her. You might scare her into silence."

The stout man looked upset. "You are ready to encourage this blackmail?"

"I want the name of that man. As soon as I have it, I'll make sure to get her address. Then you can go and question her as much as you like."

"I don't like the idea of waiting," he said.

"It's better than frightening her into running off and telling us nothing more."

"You think she might do that?"

"I'm almost certain of it."

"You'll give us her name and address as soon as you receive the information she has offered to sell you?"

"Yes. I promise."

"Why can't I be here? I can talk to her as soon as she passes the name over to you."

"I think not," she said. "We may need further information

from her. If she realizes I have placed her in your hands, she won't trust me again. But if you move in on her at another time and place, you needn't reveal that I told you about her."

The stout man rubbed his chin. "I don't like it."

"I've been frank with you," she said. "I think it only fair that you give me your cooperation."

He sighed. "All right. I'll give you another twenty-four hours. Then I want to know who the girl is and where I can reach her."

"I agree."

"And about Simpson? You'll take the risk of keeping him on?"

"Yes. I don't think it is a risk. I trust him."

"I wouldn't trust him too far," was the detective's warning. "I'll be back tomorrow morning unless you call me before. And I'll want to know all about that girl then."

"I understand," she said.

After the detective left, she considered her new problem. So Simpson was an ex-convict. It could be that he was in league with Henry in some sinister scheme against her. She had been ready to accuse old Chen of spying on her and worse, when it probably was the burly man she'd insisted on hiring whom she should fear.

The irony of it was that she'd given Simpson the letters for her parents and her children, the letters to be delivered in the event her life was taken. She wondered what he had done with them? Probably turned them over to Henry if they were fellow conspirators. It was a chilling thought.

She went to the rear window of the living room and saw Simpson working in the garden. She had believed in him, and now it seemed she had made a grievous error—though not her first, by any means. She thought that her number one mistake was when she'd married Henry Davis.

But the handsome widower had been such a different man then. There had seemed every reason why their marriage ought to be a happy one. And at first, blessed with prosperity and children, they had literally wanted for nothing. Yet the seeds of the trouble may have been germinating even then. She remembered his withdrawal when she protested about his being engaged in the opium trade. Then the mysterious visitors who had come and gone in the old mansion had increased his moodiness—until he became the bitter, nervous man who was almost a stranger to Ishbel.

Mrs. Needles appeared in the doorway of the living room to tell her, "There's a person at the door with a message for you."

"Thank you," she said. And she went to the front door to find a lad standing there with an envelope in his hand.

"Mrs. Davis?" the lad asked.

"Yes."

"I was to deliver this to you personal," the boy said with a seriousness which belied his ten or twelve years. He gave her the envelope.

As she saw him prepare to leave, she asked, "Shouldn't you wait to see if an answer is required?"

"No!" the lad said. "Man told me I wasn't to wait for an answer."

Mystified, she said, "Very well." The lad ran off and was out of sight in a few minutes. She closed the door and opened the envelope. The message was brief, "I must see you at once!" It was signed by Peter Graves.

She had almost forgotten about the artist who had been Patricia's first love. With a sigh she put the note in her pocket and sought out the housekeeper.

"I'll be out for a little," she told Mrs. Needles.

"What if your cousin comes?" the old woman wanted to know.

"Tell him I'll be back shortly," she said, "and ask him to wait."

"Very well," Mrs. Needles said, sounding disgruntled.

Ishbel went up and tidied her hair and put on a bonnet. Then she made her way downstairs and out. She walked the half-circle of Castle Square to the house of the artist at Number Twenty-Eight, used the door rapper, and waited.

Peter opened the door himself. The well-dressed young man wore a gray frock coat, beige vest and trousers a shade lighter than his vest. He stood back to let her in. "Thank you for being so prompt."

"Your message sounded urgent," she said, going inside.

"I wasn't even sure you'd be at home," he said, escorting her into the living room.

"I've been home all morning. I had a call from Detective Hawker," she said.

The artist showed interest. "What did he want?"

"He came to tell me Simpson is an ex-convict."

"The fishmonger fellow whom you hired to replace Griffin?"

"Yes," she said grimly. "The one I trusted completely."

Peter Graves eyed her in a mocking fashion. "Rather a rough joke on you."

"It is news that I would have preferred not to hear."

He said, "Sit down, won't you? Have a sherry?"

She sat in one of the several easy chairs. "I don't think so."

The artist was at the sideboard already pouring out the drinks. "I think you'd better have one. It will help steady your nerves."

"Why did you want to see me?" she asked.

He came to her and gave her a glass of sherry. "This is

163

really very good," he assured her as he sipped some from his own glass.

She took a sip of the sherry. "Why did you call me over here?"

He gulped down the rest of his sherry and stared at his glass. "Where is Henry?"

"My husband went to Liverpool," she said.

"Are you sure?"

Uneasily, she said, "Why do you ask?"

"I merely want to know. Are you certain that he has gone to Liverpool?"

Further confused, she said, "I can only say that he packed his valise and left the house late yesterday afternoon. He told me that he was leaving by stage for Liverpool."

Peter Graves was staring at her in a strange way. "I think he lied to you."

"Why?"

"Because I saw him leaving the Westminster Hotel in London last night in the company of a ghost. He was entering a cab with a young woman. And the young woman was Patricia!"

Chapter Nine

Though Ishbel had harbored serious doubts as to whether her husband was going to Liverpool, she was ill-prepared for this shattering account by Peter Graves. She could only sit in stunned silence for a moment.

Then in a low voice she asked, "Are you sure?"

"I would swear to it," he said with a deep sigh. "Unhappily, I wasn't able to prove it. He and the woman were in the cab and off before I could find another cab in which to follow them."

"I see," she said.

He began to pace back and forth before her. "All I could think about when I saw them together was what you'd told me that foggy night. You assured me you'd had a glimpse of Patricia. Of course I doubted you."

"Now you think differently."

"I have to," he said. "And yet I can't understand it. I can't imagine Patricia alive. Nor can I guess why she and Henry would be together if she were alive."

Ishbel told him, "Lawyer Slade is convinced he saw her as well—standing outside Number Twenty-Two. It gave him a great shock."

"Nor more than the one I received last night," the artist said. "I couldn't wait to tell you about it."

She said, "What can it mean?"

"I wish I knew."

She gave him a questioning glance. "Do you know anyone whose name begins with 'L'?" she asked.

He halted his pacing to stare at her. "Probably a dozen or

more people. Why do you ask?"

"I'm thinking of someone who would also know Patricia."

"That narrows it," the artist said. After a moment, he said, "There was a Lawrence Gale. But he is living in Germany now."

"It's not apt to be he."

"What about this 'L'?" Peter asked.

"Patricia wrote a note to him the night of her death," Ishbel said.

"Go on!"

"In the note she hinted that Henry knew of her betraying him with another man. And she said that she feared for her life. Within a few hours she'd suffered that fall down the stairs."

Peter Graves showed interest. "How did you find this out?"

"Did you ever hear of Clara Sawyer?"

"Yes. She was Patricia's personal maid. I understand Henry dismissed her shortly after Patricia's death."

"That is so," she agreed. "Clara Sawyer came to me to bargain, to sell me information. I bought that letter from her."

The artist gasped. "Had she anything else to offer?"

"Yes. Tonight she is bringing me the name and address of the lover whom Patricia was seeing at the time of her death."

"I find that hard to believe!" the artist said, shocked.

"I have made a bargain with her," she said. "And I'm of the opinion she means to keep her word."

Peter Graves frowned. "I never wanted to think Patricia had another lover aside from me. But it is probable I was wrong. I'd say that once you get the name of her lover, we will have a much better chance of tracking down the phantom."

"If it should be a phantom," she qualified.

"I'm too mixed up now to be sure of anything," the artist complained.

"I'm in the same position," she said bitterly. "My husband is not only a possible murderer; it also seems that he has been blatantly unfaithful to me."

The artist said, "Maybe we should combine our misery. I find myself desperately lonely at the moment."

"I mean to discover the truth before I make any plans for the future," she said.

"How does one find the truth in a situation like this?" he wanted to know.

"I'm not sure," she said worriedly. And then she went on to tell him of her visitation by the phantom Patricia the night before.

"And you fired the pistol at her directly?"

"Yes," she said. "But afterwards there was no sign of her having been hurt."

"What harm does a bullet do a phantom?"

"I think I fired wildly. The phantom may be more flesh and blood than you guess."

Peter Graves said, "All right! Let us admit the unlikely and say she is still alive. What are she and Henry doing together?"

"It has to be that she is an opium addict and she is managing to blackmail Henry into keeping her supplied with the drug."

"How is she managing it?"

"Henry may have tried to kill her and she is holding that over his head."

"I wish it wouldn't all fit so well," the artist said unhappily. "I want it to be different."

"You don't want Patricia alive?"

"I have come to doubt my eyes," he admitted. "I can't believe it possible."

Ishbel rose. "I have some more evidence as to its likelihood. Last night I went to visit her father."

"Lord Carney?"

"Yes."

"He sees no one. How did you manage it?"

"Lawyer Slade and he are old friends. He gave me a letter to take to him."

"And?"

"I talked with the old man."

"Did he tell you anything?"

"He would not discuss Patricia's burial or show me where she is buried. He mentioned the family vault, but when I asked to see her casket, he gave me a point blank refusal."

"Strange," Peter Graves said. "Very strange."

She said, "I'm expecting my cousin, Ernest, so I must be on my way."

"You do have some relatives in London?"

"He is here only temporarily in the interests of the family bank in Edinburgh. Still, I'm glad to have him here at this time."

"I realize that," Peter Graves said. "You will let me know what evidence the Clara Sawyer girl brings you."

"I will."

"Have you told the police about her?"

"Yes. They have agreed not to move in against her until after she visits me tonight. Then they will also try and get additional information from her."

Peter Graves looked glum. "I hope this is all to good purpose. I would not like to see Patricia's name smeared and nothing gained by it. She escaped scandal in life, and one would hope that she might be equally fortunate in death."

"If she is dead," Ishbel reminded him.

"I find that hard to think about," he said.

"So do I. But it must be faced. Just as I must accept that my husband is a good deal less than I hoped."

"This means your marriage is in a ruin. What will you do?"

She shrugged. "Return to Edinburgh and raise my children there, I suppose."

"Have you not come to like London?"

"Not enough to live here alone."

Peter Graves smiled bitterly. "The Stewarts of Stormhaven! Isn't that how they refer to your family in Edinburgh?"

"Only my Uncle Walter lives at Stormhaven now," she said. "He is the one member of the family identified with it these days."

She left Number Twenty-Eight with the promise that she would keep the artist informed. Then she started to hurry back to her own house, but she was halted by the remarkable sight of the door of Twenty-Six opening and old Lawyer Slade appearing in the open doorway, leaning on his cane to favor his gouty foot.

Ishbel halted with a gasp. "I had no idea you could get around so well."

The old man said crankily, "I don't, usually. But I saw from the window that you were calling on Graves. And I had not heard from you since I gave you the letter to Lord Carney. I decided to intercept you on the way back. It seemed my only hope of hearing from you."

"I'm sorry," she said, moving up the steps to him. "I meant to come see you later. I only visited Peter Graves because he sent me a message."

"A message?"

"Yes." And she proceeded to tell him what the artist had told her.

"It has to be a ghost!" Lawyer Slade declared. "We have

all seen her, yet we know she's dead."

"I have seen her twice," she informed the old lawyer. "Once outside in the fog and then again last night. She appeared in my bedroom and I fired a shot at her. She vanished."

The old man's mouth gaped open. "A ghost!" he murmured. "She cannot rest easily in her grave!"

"Ghosts rarely visit the Westminster Hotel in the company of their former husbands," she said with irony.

"What then?"

"Patricia must be somehow alive or there is a look-alike whom we are taking for her."

"There could be no such look-alike unless she had a twin. And she was Carney's only child."

"Sometimes one meets a double," Ishbel insisted. And she quickly filled in the old man about Simpson being a former convict and about the information she was receiving from Clara Sawyer.

The old lawyer exclaimed, "Surely the police have enough to solve this mystery now. Why should you place yourself in additional danger?"

"I want to do my part."

"You already have."

She gave the old man a sad look. "Despite everything, I still cling to the hope that Henry may not be entirely a villain. That he is not deceiving me as it seems he must be."

"A slim hope."

"I cling to it."

"You must be prepared for the unpleasant," the old man warned her.

"I know that," she said. "But if he and Patricia were at such odds before her supposed death, they cannot truly be close to each other now."

"That makes sense," Lawyer Slade agreed. "And you were not able to get any satisfaction from Carney as to where she was buried?"

"None."

"Carney is not an easy man to deal with," the old lawyer confirmed.

"I will let you know as soon as I find anything else out," Ishbel promised.

She went on home, and when Mrs. Needles greeted her at the door it was with the news that Ernest had arrived. She said, "Your cousin is here, ma'am. He is out in the garden with Simpson."

"Very well," she said. "I'll go out to him."

It was a warm day, and Simpson was trimming an area of shrubbery with huge scissors while Ernest stood by chatting with him. When Ishbel approached the two, Ernest came to meet her with a smile and Simpson removed his cap.

She and Ernest kissed and she said, "I see you have met Simpson."

Ernest showed a smile on his pleasant face. "Yes. I find him a remarkable fellow. Fought with Nelson! Not too many around who can claim that."

Ishbel turned to Simpson and said, "You have had a remarkable career, I'm sure."

The old man with the black eye patch looked a trifle uneasy as he replied, "I suppose some would say that, ma'am."

She told Ernest, "He was a fishmonger when I first met him. I felt he would be good with the garden, and he has worked wonders out here."

Ernest said, "Hard work is the answer! It's the same in the banking business."

"I have a great deal to tell you," she told Ernest. And she

led him a distance away from Simpson to the other side of the garden. There she continued, "I have only just learned that Simpson is an ex-convict. He spent a term in prison for violent assault."

Ernest showed surprise. "He seems such a nice old chap!"

"I think he is all right," she agreed. "He was probably the victim of some misfortune. People do make mistakes and regret them."

"Exactly," the young man said. "What is your problem? Your message seemed urgent."

"Things have been happening at a fast rate here," she said. And she told him about the way in which her husband had changed, the appearance of a phantom Patricia and the doubts she was beginning to have about Patricia's death. She ended with the revelation that Clara Sawyer was bringing her the name of the man who had been Patricia's lover.

Ernest listened carefully. Then, he said, "If you get his name and can locate him, it may solve much of what is still a mystery."

"That is my hope," she said. "As far as I know, Henry is still in Liverpool. I want to learn as much as I can while he is still out of the city."

"But if he lied to you, he may still be in London," her young cousin pointed out.

"I must take that chance," she said. "I need you to help me find this mystery man after I get his name from Clara Sawyer."

"I am at your service," he promised. "And I have some other encouraging news."

"Tell me!"

"Uncle Walter is arriving in London tomorrow on bank business, and he is bringing Dr. Jock Gregory with him."

"That is good news," she said.

Ernest nodded. "I'd say so. Uncle Walter is a clever man.

His advice is bound to be good. And even though Dr. Gregory is now eighty-four-years old, he still has a keen mind and a way of ferreting out information."

"I'll be happy to see both of them again," she said. "I only wish I were in less trouble."

"They'll be glad to help you in any way they can," Ernest assured her.

"I think you can be of the most use," she said. "I can't very well ask two elderly men to comb the avenues and alleys of London looking for some mysterious person."

"When do we begin?" Ernest asked.

"Tonight," she said. "Clara Sawyer should arrive about eight o'clock. As soon as I get the name and address from her, we can begin our search."

"Very well," Ernest said, taking out his pocket watch. "Suppose I arrive here at nine with a hansom cab. We'll need transportation."

"Excellent," she said. "I'll not forget your kindness."

"We Stewarts must help one another," he said. "I only hope it turns out that Henry is not as guilty as it seems."

"So do I," she said. "But I have no choice now. I must find out the whole truth."

Ernest went back to the bank, and she was left to spend the day alone. She went upstairs to her room and made sure the pistol was still in the lower drawer, hidden beneath the blankets. Then she stretched out on the bed for a rest, since she had not slept well during the night.

When she wakened it was early afternoon. She went back downstairs and encountered the black-clad Chen in the hallway. She asked him, "Did anyone come by while I was resting?"

"No, missee," he said. "There have been no callers."

"The house is very warm," she complained. "Have you

173

opened all the windows you can?"

"It is a hot day, missee," Chen replied. "Perhaps storm is on the way."

"It is most unusual weather," she said. "It is never like this in Scotland."

She had the venerable Chen bring her tea and cakes, which she enjoyed in the back parlor, where there was a small breeze. She had forgotten to ask Ernest the exact time when he expected their Uncle Walter and Dr. Jock Gregory to arrive. She wanted to see them as soon as possible and have their sage advice in the crisis she was facing.

The hours went by with maddening slowness. Her tension rose as the evening approached. She ate little dinner and then sat down in the rear parlor to wait the appearance of Clara Sawyer. She had little doubt that the mercenary maid would want to collect her ten pounds. She only hoped that the girl didn't try to trick her by giving her a made-up name. It seemed odd that she hadn't brought all the information with her the previous night, but perhaps Clara had felt she could get a better deal this way.

Eight o'clock came, and there was no sign of the maid. Ishbel now found herself worrying that Henry might return home unexpectedly and meet the girl whom he had dismissed from service. Soon it was eight-fifteen, and then the half-hour approached. She decided that the girl had lost her nerve and would not return.

Then there was a gentle knock on the door. She went and opened it to find Clara Sawyer standing there. She said, "I had almost given you up."

The girl entered the room with a nervous air. "I think I was followed here," she said.

"Who would follow you?" Ishbel asked.

"Him," Clara said.

"You mean my husband?"

"Yes."

"He is supposed to be in Liverpool until tomorrow."

Clara was in a bad mood. "Someone followed me. I could feel it." As she finished speaking, there was a loud rumble of thunder outside, and a bright flash of lightning shot in through the windows of the room.

"We're going to have a storm," Ishbel said.

"I have no cloak," the girl lamented.

"I'll let you have one of mine," she told her. "Did you bring the name?"

"I have it memorized," the girl said. "Do you have the ten pounds?"

"Yes. Here's the money."

The girl took the bank notes and thrust them in her pocket. Then she said, "His name is Reginald Garth, and he lives in a flat at 40 Portland Road. That is where the missus used to go meet him."

"I'll write it down," Ishbel said, going to the nearby table and finding a pencil and paper. As she wrote down the name, she said, "Where exactly is it?"

There was another heavy roar of thunder and a jarring flash of lightning following it. The girl waited for a few seconds to answer. As it began to pour rain she said, "I have never been there, but I know the house is in a court in the East End, not far from the docks."

Ishbel had the slip of paper with the name and address written on it as she turned to face the girl. "I assume it would be a dangerous place for a woman to venture alone."

"No doubt of that, ma'am," the maid said. "The missus only went there when she was sure Garth would come partway to meet her. Once he did not turn up, and she came back weeping. She was afraid to go on alone."

"What do you think made her go to such a dreadful place with a man who wasn't reliable?"

"Opium, ma'am," Clara Sawyer said. "I know for a fact that she and that man smoked opium together. She told me what a glorious sleepy feeling it gave her and how, after he fell into a drugged sleep, she used to try to get extra satisfaction from the ashes left in his pipe."

"Do you think her husband knew about this?"

"He had to have known something was wrong. He didn't want me talking about it to anyone. That was why he discharged me."

Ishbel said, "I'll get you a cloak."

"Thank you, ma'am," the girl said. The rain was coming in a torrent now.

Ishbel brought her a cloak from the hall closet. It was one that gave excellent protection from the rain and that she had used often. She said, "You will find this will keep most of the rain off."

"Thank you, ma'am," the girl said throwing it over her shoulders.

"You can stay here for a little longer until the rain eases, if you like," Ishbel suggested.

"No," Clara said quickly. "I want to be on my way. I don't want to be on the streets too late."

"Just as you say."

"I'll leave by the side door, same as I came in," the girl said starting out. At the door she turned and said, "Don't ever tell him I gave you the name of that man and all. He'll kill me if he finds out."

"I won't say a word to him," she promised.

"Thank you, ma'am. Be careful!" the girl said. Then she opened the door and hurried out.

By this time it was nearly nine o'clock and pitch dark.

Ishbel gazed out at the downpour of rain and wondered if Ernest would abandon the project because of the storm. She hoped not. Now that she had the actual name and address of the man who had been Patricia's lover, she wanted to try and locate him without delay.

Mrs. Needles came to inform her, "Your cousin has arrived, Mrs. Davis."

"Yes," she said, the slip of paper in her hand. "I'm going out with him."

"In this rain?"

"Yes. We must make a certain call. Will you go upstairs and get my heavy cloak?"

"I will, ma'am," the housekeeper grumbled. "But I don't see why you can't put the call off until another night."

Ernest had almost the same opinion to offer when she joined him in the front hall. Her cousin was wearing a raincoat with a short cape attached to give him extra protection from the downpour. He said, "It's a miserable night. Do you think we should change our plans?"

"Never," she said, holding up the slip. "I have the name and the address."

"Where is it?"

"Portland Road. In the East End and near the docks."

Ernest gave a low whistle. "I haven't been in London long, but I have heard enough to know that is a bad section. I say it's too dangerous for you. Let me go seek out this man on my own."

"No," she said. "I'm not afraid. Patricia went there regularly. I've as much courage as she had."

"By all accounts this Patricia was more than a little mad."

"An opium addict. I have it on the word of her personal maid."

"But it is different with you," Ernest said.

"My need to find the truth is as compelling as her drug addiction," she said. "I have no choice. I must find that man and question him."

"Very well," Ernest said with a shrug.

Mrs. Needles came down the stairs and helped Ishbel put on the cloak. The old woman grumbled about her going out in the bad weather. "The master wouldn't allow it if he were at home," she averred.

Ishbel gave the wrinkled housekeeper a wan smile. "But he isn't at home. I'll return as soon as I can. I may be late."

"There will be someone to let you in," Mrs. Needles told her. "Even if it is only that heathen Chen!"

They dodged out of the house and across the sidewalk to the waiting carriage. The driver, perched up in back with a cape to shelter him from the rain, opened the slot at the rear of the carriage to receive the address from Ernest.

When he heard the address the driver said, "Portland Road, Guv'nor? You can't be serious. You don't want to go there tonight!"

"We must go there," Ernest shouted up to him.

"It could be worth your life," the driver complained. "I have known throats to be cut there for half a sovereign!"

"Can't be helped," Ernest said. "40 Portland Road is where you must take us."

"I'll drive you as far as the court, but I won't venture inside. You can find the house on your own. I'll wait in the road if you like."

"Just get us there," Ernest shouted and then closed the slot against the rain. The driver cursed loudly enough to be heard by them inside; then he roused his miserable, drenched horse into action, and they started off over the wet cobblestones.

"I'm sorry to have dragged you into this," Ishbel apologized.

Ernest took her hands in his. "What are cousins for but to share troubles?"

"You have been so good to me, Ernest."

"I only ask that you stay in the carriage and wait for me while I explore this court and try to find the Garth fellow."

"I will not allow you to go alone," she said firmly.

"But your being with me could make it more dangerous for both of us," he warned her.

"I very much doubt that," she replied.

The carriage rattled over the wet cobblestones, lurching this way and that. Outside the rain still poured down, and she marveled that the driver could find his way with only the swinging lantern hanging from the front of the carriage to give him light.

London was an eerie, dark place on this stormy night. Occasionally they passed the lighted entrance of a tavern or a shop. The occasional corner gas lamp gave a small glow against the blackness. And every so often another carriage came rattling by, its lantern swinging and its driver crying out imprecations against the storm, the uneven streets and his horse!

As they reached the poorer section of the city, there were scarcely any carriages, and the tavern lights became more infrequent. Fortunately the rain had slowed down to a drizzle. At last the carriage came to a halt. The driver opened the slot and in his hoarse voice shouted, "This is where it begins. The entrance to the court is over on the right!"

"Good," Ernest said. Then he peered out the window and murmured, "Doesn't seem to be anything there but a lot of rubble."

"The courtyard must be somewhere beyond the rubble," Ishbel insisted.

"Well, no point in delaying any longer," Ernest said and

got out. He helped Ishbel down into the street, and she held her cloak tight around her to fend off the cold drizzle.

The driver bent down. "I'll have my fare now, sir. The half-pound you promised me."

Ernest said, "How do I know you'll wait for us if I pay you?"

The driver had a heavy black mustache, and water dripped down from its ends. "How do I know you'll come back alive if you go in there?"

Ishbel groaned. "Give him his money. Don't let us stand here arguing."

"All right," Ernest said with some annoyance. He found the money and handed it up to the driver. "Mind you wait for us, now. I'll pay you an extra half-pound for taking us back."

"I'll wait," the mustached one in the top hat said gloomily. "But I never risked my neck for a bleedin' pound note before!"

Ishbel clung to her cousin's arm. She said, "You didn't find us a very cheerful driver."

"Lucky to find anyone willing to come down here at this time of night in a storm," he said.

Her eyes were becoming accustomed to the darkness now, and she pointed ahead. "There's an entrance over there. That must be where the courtyard is."

"I wish we were back in Edinburgh," Ernest said unhappily as they started forward.

They stayed close together as they headed for the courtyard. Suddenly out of the darkness a scarecrow, tallish man came staggering. He was singing some sort of sea-chanty, but he was far too advanced in drunkenness to be coherent. The words were lost and the tune was distressingly off-key. He lurched by them, leaving a strong odor of gin in his wake.

Ishbel was trembling and her fear was rising in her throat,

but she said nothing. She did not want to let Ernest guess that she was terrified, she who had talked him into this mad adventure. As they reached the entrance to the court, Ernest stumbled over something that he declared was a dead cat.

Now she was aware of the rows of wretched houses around them. None of them were any better than shanties. She found herself wondering how any of them could be dignified by a number. Had Clara Sawyer played a trick on her after all?

A door opened close by them on the left, and a woman shoved a man out, uttering shrill imprecations after him. The man cursed her back and shook his fist at her as the door of the shanty banged closed.

"Tykes your money and throws you out," the man cried in a jeering tone. Then he turned and almost ran into them. "Gor' Blimey!" he gasped.

"It's all right. We're trying to find someone," Ernest told him.

"You've come to a rotten place for it," the man warned him. He was short and had a battered face and was dressed in rags.

"Maybe you can help us," Ishbel said.

"Any way I can, miss. I'm not one to turn me back on a lady," the man said in a manner which made her more uneasy.

Ernest said, "Let me handle this." He reached in his pocket and brought out some coins, which he gave to the man. "Where is Number Forty?"

"I don't know, guv'nor," the man said. "No one pays much heed to numbers here."

"Do you know a man called Reginald Garth?" Ishbel asked.

"Garth?" the man repeated.

Ernest said, "He is supposed to live at Number Forty, but

he may stay here only at certain times. It is likely he's from the other part of the city."

This seemed to make an impression on the man. He said, "You mean the toff who comes down here to hit the pipe and brings the judy with him?"

"That sounds like him," Ishbel agreed.

"Now he's a rare one, miss! We just see him now and again, and the judy is only with him part of the time. But she's a real beauty! You don't see her like down here!"

"Which house?" Ernest asked impatiently.

"Right over there," the man said, pointing.

"Thank you," Ernest said grimly. And to Ishbel, "Come along and let us get this over with!"

"Any time I can help, guv'nor!" the man shouted after them.

"What sort of man would bring Patricia down here?" she wondered.

"A man who wanted to smoke opium without being interfered with or recognized," her cousin said. "And that is why she came here as well. It was a place to lose themselves in their vice!"

"Horrible!" she said with a shudder. And she wondered what guilt her husband must feel, dealing in the drug as he did.

They crossed the muddy, uneven courtyard and came to a house that looked much like all the others. Rickety steps led to a slanted door. They mounted the steps and pounded on the door.

After a long while it was opened a crack, and someone holding a candle peered out at them. A hoarse voice, which could have been either male or female asked, "What is it?"

Ernest said, "We're looking for Reginald Garth."

The presence behind the door hesitated and said, "No one of that name here!"

Ernest lunged at the door and forced it open. A frightened old harridan stumbled back, still managing to hold the candle in her hand. Her wasted features showed a look of hatred as she bared toothless gums to snarl, "You can't rob me! I've nothing for you to take!"

Ernest said, "We don't want to rob you. We want to find Garth. Where is he?"

"Not here!" the old woman quavered, shrinking back with her shadow looming over her on the wall and wavering with the glow of the candle.

Ernest said, "Where is he?"

"I don't know. He comes when he likes and goes when he likes," the old woman said.

Ishbel said, "What about the girl?"

The old woman eyed her uneasily. "She left with him."

"When?"

"This morning. They were both here last night, but they left this morning."

Ernest and Ishbel exchanged glances. Then Ernest asked the old woman, "When do they usually come back?"

"No telling," she said. "Who are you? What do you want with them?"

"The girl is related to me," Ishbel said, not exactly accurately. "I want to help her."

"She don't need help!" the old woman snapped. "They have plenty!"

"I want to stop her from coming down here and smoking opium," Ishbel said.

The old woman's rheumy eyes were filled with hatred. "I don't ask my lodgers what they do! I don't interfere with them! I don't know anything about opium smoking!"

"They don't come down here for the atmosphere," Ernest told her. "What does Garth look like?"

"A big man. Wears a black patch over his eye," the old woman said. "And he'd soon settle you if he were here!"

"What about the girl?" Ishbel asked.

"She's a beauty—" the old woman said venomously. "—a whole lot prettier than you!"

Ernest said, "I think we'd better get away from here. This is a job for the police."

"All right," Ishbel acquiesced, filled with despair. Their quarry had fled, and they had learned very little for all their trouble—except the description of the man as wearing a black eye patch! It fitted Simpson! But who would describe him as a toff? Perhaps he might seem one to the wretches in this place! Still she couldn't picture Patricia being mixed up with him.

They left the old woman, who shouted after them, "No need to bring the police! I've done nothing against the law!"

Ernest was jumpy as he hurried his cousin along across the muddy terrain. "Let's get back to the carriage as quickly as possible," he told Ishbel.

They hurried on, stumbling and supporting each other. At last the opening to the wider street beyond showed ahead. It would only be a moment or two before they were back in the carriage.

Then Ishbel screamed, "Look out!" as three dark figures bore down upon them!

Chapter Ten

Ernest was quick to heed her warning. As the first of the thugs sprang forward to attack him, he sent a crashing blow into the man's face that sent him toppling back. By this time another assailant had come up behind the young man to try to pin down his arms. As Ernest flailed around and escaped this attempt, the tallest of the thugs pressed in and struck him hard on the temple!

Ernest reeled. Ishbel screamed again and tried to rush to his rescue, but the tall thug grasped her and threw her aside, and she went tumbling down into the mud. At the same time the other two attackers closed in on Ernest. Ishbel cried out again and somehow got to her feet.

It seemed the drama taking place in the black courtyard was about to reach a climax with Ernest being beaten and robbed. Ishbel did not dare think what might happen to her. It was at this darkest moment of despair that a whistle suddenly sounded in the opening to the court. As Ishbel heard the sound, which was repeated twice, she saw three newcomers racing towards them.

The sound of the whistle had a magical effect on the three thugs. They exchanged warning shouts and then ran for cover in the courtyard of hovels. Two of the newcomers chased after them, while the third man halted to speak to her and Ernest.

"You see what comes of not confiding in the police," a familiar voice came through to Ishbel in spite of her near-fainting state. She recognized it as belonging to Detective Hawker.

Still breathing hard, Ernest said, "You arrived just in the

nick of time! They had me nearly finished!"

"Are either of you hurt badly?" the Detective wanted to know. "Those thugs are handy with knives!"

Ishbel said, "I'm all right except for being thrown in the mud."

"So am I," Ernest gasped, "except for a few bruises and a missing top hat."

"You'd best chalk that top hat off to experience," the stout detective said dryly.

"How did you know we were here?" Ishbel asked.

He chuckled. "You didn't think you'd put me off completely, did you? I've had men watching the house all evening. And when you and this young man came out and got in the carriage, we followed you. I counted on your leading us to where the man in the case would be found."

She said, "We found his lodging place, but he wasn't there!"

"We'll worry about that later," the detective said, "just now I want to get you and the young man out of here safely." He blew on his whistle again.

Ishbel told the detective, "The man's name is Reginald Garth, and he and Patricia have been meeting here. In fact, the old woman who rented them the rooms for their opium smoking orgies claims they were both here earlier today."

Ernest said, "Which has to mean that Patricia is still alive."

"It could," Detective Hawker agreed. And when his two men came back to join them, he asked, "What about those three?"

"They got away," one of the bobbies in uniform told him. "Slunk back into their hiding places like the vermin they are!"

"They aren't important," Detective Hawker said. "What we have to do now is check on a lodging place." He turned to

Ishbel. "Which of these hovels is it?"

"Number Forty," she said. "It's directly in the middle of the far row of houses. An old woman is the proprietor. You will find it hard to get much information from her."

"We'll make a good try!" the detective said grimly. And to his men he added, "You come with me, Moore. Let Benson take these two back to their carriage!"

Ishbel asked, "Shall we wait in the carriage?"

"No," the detective said. "This is a dangerous district. Get away from here as soon as you can. I'll visit you in the morning with any information I'm able to pry from the landlady."

There was no arguing with his tone of authority. They meekly followed the uniformed bobby out of the courtyard, while the old detective and the other bobby went on to interview the harridan who'd rented rooms to the mysterious Reginald Garth and Patricia.

The cabman was pacing up and down by his carriage as he waited for them. When he had a good look at their condition, his doleful, mustached face took on an expression of shock. "I knew you two wouldn't come to any good going in there! They bashed you properly, didn't they?"

"Not so much guff!" the bobby said sternly. "Take them directly back to Castle Square."

Not until they were in the carriage and on their way back to Number Twenty-Two did Ishbel realize what a fantastic experience they'd gone through. She shuddered as she thought of their narrow escape. The three thugs who'd attacked them were easily capable of slitting their throats for the sake of their money and clothing. Their bodies would have been thrown in some sewer and they would simply have vanished.

Ernest gave her a concerned glance. "Are you feeling some better?"

"Yes. What about you?"

"I'll survive."

"I'm terrified to think what might have happened!" she said with awe.

"Don't talk about it," he chided her. "You couldn't be happy until we went down there."

"I felt we had to do it."

"You might as well have let the police come with us in the first place. They followed us anyway."

"I didn't know that. I worried that we might find Henry there, and I wanted to give him a chance to explain."

"Still trying to protect that precious husband of yours, who apparently spends most of his time skulking around with his phantom first wife!"

"We don't know that!"

"It sounds mighty like it," Ernest said. "We were lucky that detective fellow came along."

"I am grateful."

"You mustn't attempt any more investigating on your own!" Ernest warned her.

The carriage rolled along in the drizzle of rain, the night still black. Ishbel was absorbed with her thoughts to the point that she was hardly aware of her disheveled state. She finally turned to the young man seated beside her.

"Do you remember what that old woman said?"

Ernest shrugged. "She said a lot of things."

"She told us the man called Reginald Garth wore a black eye patch."

"So?"

"Don't you remember someone with a black eye patch? Someone you recently talked with at Castle Square?"

His eyebrows raised. "Simpson!"

"Exactly!"

"You think this Garth might be him?"

"I find it hard to believe. But the description fits."

"It could fit many men. There are lots of black eye patches being worn in London. I think Nelson made them popular."

She sighed. "Still, it makes you wonder. Simpson is an ex-convict."

"Let the detective deal with it," Ernest protested. "I'm too weary to think about it. Uncle Walter and Dr. Gregory will be arriving in the morning, and I'll be in fine shape to greet them. Probably both my eyes are blacked."

"I'll explain that you were helping me," she promised.

"That won't improve their opinion of my judgment," he worried. "Bankers are supposed to be the epitome of respectability."

"Do you think Patricia is alive?" she asked, to change the subject.

"That old woman said she showed up regularly with Garth."

"I know. I was shocked to hear her say that Patricia had been there earlier."

"You've half-believed she was alive from the very start," Ernest said.

"Where does Henry fit in the picture?" she worried.

"Could he be Garth?"

She gave her cousin a frightened glance. "That thought came to you as well?"

"Why not? He may simply be using the eye patch to be sure he isn't recognized. It makes a great change of identity. People's attention is drawn to the eye patch rather than to the whole face."

Ishbel sat back against the carriage seat. "It should soon be over. We soon ought to know the truth."

Ernest became sympathetic, saying, "Forgive me for complaining as I did. This is an ordeal for you. I hope it doesn't turn out too badly. Perhaps Henry is mixed up in whatever is going on only in a minor way."

"I pray that is so," she sighed.

"I wouldn't worry too much before hand."

"I've done nothing but worry these past weeks. That is why I sent the children to Scotland—to get them away from the poisonous atmosphere at Number Twenty-Two."

"The detective has promised to see you in the morning," he said. "I have an idea he's a clever old chap. He surely came at the right moment tonight."

When they arrived back at Castle Square, Ernest saw her safely to her door, and Chen was on hand to let her in. Ernest said, "As soon as I've talked with Uncle Walter and Dr. Gregory I'll come back here and see you. They should arrive on the early stage in the morning."

"Thank you," she said. "You have been most kind."

"No more so than I should be," Ernest said. "Now go to bed and try to rest."

She went inside and inquired of Chen about Simpson. She asked, "Do you know if the gardener has been out this evening?"

The old Chinese eyed her blandly. "No, missee."

"Have you any idea if he was away from here earlier in the day?"

Chen nodded vigorously. "He went somewhere this morning."

This fitted and made her worry more. "Thank you," she told Chen. And she went up the dark stairway to the bedroom she would occupy alone until Henry returned . . . *if* he returned! This was a dreadful thought. Suppose he should run off with the reincarnated Patricia somewhere!

She found the pistol in the dresser drawer, and when she

went to bed it was under her pillow. Her dress and cloak were covered with dirty slime and so were her shoes. Everything would need a thorough cleaning. She bathed as best she could in the cold water in her room. In the morning she would rise early and have a warm bath. She would see that the maid brought her an extra jug of hot water. She lay back and closed her eyes and was soon asleep from sheer weariness.

The maid wakened her the next morning when she arrived with the regular jug of water. The girl saw the clothes hung over a chair and the scandalous condition of them.

Gasping, she said, "Were you caught in the storm, ma'am?"

"Worse than that," Ishbel said. "Take the things down-stairs and see they are cleaned. And bring me another jug of hot water. I intend to take a long, warm bath."

"Yes, ma'am," the girl said, gathering up the soiled clothing and finally the shoes. "It was a desperate storm, and now the fog is back this morning."

"Is it really?" Ishbel said. "I hadn't noticed."

"It's real thick, ma'am," the maid said at the door. "I'll be back in a few minutes with more water."

Ishbel felt refreshed after a good, long, hot bath. Then she went downstairs for breakfast. She had barely finished when Mrs. Needles came into the dining room to inform her, "That detective person is here to see you again. What shall I say?"

Ishbel touched her napkin to her lips. "Tell him I'll be right out."

"Very well, ma'am," Mrs. Needles said and started to leave.

Ishbel asked her, "Is Simpson around?"

"Yes," the housekeeper said. "He had breakfast with us early, and now he's out working in the toolshed. He tells wicked tales of his adventures in the navy. He has the younger maids blushing and squealing by turns."

Mrs. Needles went on out, and Ishbel took a few sips more
of tea. She had the feeling that the morning ahead would be
one of revelations. She'd wanted to be sure Simpson was
available if Detective Hawker wished to call on him. She did
not think he could be Reginald Garth, but at the same time he
did wear an eye patch and he had been away yesterday
morning on some errand. Perhaps he left the house more than
anyone noticed.

When she entered the living room, Detective Hawker was
sitting rather awkwardly in a tall-backed chair. He rose at
once. "Good morning," he said. "I see you've rid yourself of a
deal of London mud!"

She smiled wanly. "I'm afraid I've left my wash-woman to
deal with the worst of it."

"No matter," he said. "You are safe and none the worse
for your experience."

"We can thank you for that."

"When Sir Robert Peel formed the force, it was for the
protection of all," the stout man said with a serious look on
his round face. "I'm no more than doing my duty."

"What have you found out?"

"Please, sit down," Detective Hawker suggested. "I have a
few things to go over. It will take some time."

She seated herself on a nearby chair. "You saw the old
woman?"

"And a harridan she turned out to be! Runs that filthy
hovel of a lodging house and deals in stolen goods on the
side!"

"What did you find out about Reginald Garth and the
woman who joins him there?"

"I was shown the rooms they have on regular rental.
Hardly any furniture in them, save some mattresses on the

floor and them none too clean at that! I found a hidden cache of opium, pipes and all the rest. They used the place solely to indulge their vice."

She said, "I did not expect it to be a luxury apartment."

"According to the old woman, they met there three or maybe four times a week—sometimes in the day, and then they would come once in a while and remain all the night. And there were months at a time when she saw neither of them; this made them desirable tenants in her eyes!"

"What about Reginald Garth?"

"All I could get out of her was that he spoke like a toff and had plenty of money. She also mentioned that he wore a black eye patch."

"Like Simpson," she said.

"Like Simpson," Detective Hawker agreed. "But then Simpson doesn't talk like a gentleman, does he? I have always thought his speech rather coarse—the voice of a fishmonger, hoarse from his shouting in the streets!"

"So you would rule out Simpson?"

"For the moment."

"I'm glad," she said. "I think the poor old man is innocent of any wrongdoing in this case."

"The alternate possibility is not pleasant," Detective Hawker warned her. "There is a chance that Reginald Garth could be your husband, Henry Davis, using an assumed identity."

"I've been tormented by that all along," she admitted. "His strange behavior and his mysterious disappearances; the people who have come here at night, especially the woman; and his denial of the visits—all these things have tended to make me fear the worst about him."

"Yet you don't want to believe it," the stout detective said.

"No. In spite of everything, I still love my husband."

"That is admirable of you, ma'am. I trust your belief in him will be justified."

"Even now he is absent, supposedly in Liverpool. But our neighbor, the artist Peter Graves, claims he saw him in London the night he was supposed to have left."

Detective Hawker showed interest. "We will check on that."

"Isn't there a chance that this Reginald Garth is a person in his own right? Some villainous creature who through being a fellow drug addict gained control of Patricia."

"I do not rule that out," Detective Hawker told her. "I'm trying to establish whether there is a real Reginald Garth or not at this very moment. Several of my men are working on it."

"He isn't apt to return to that lodging house, is he?"

"I'm sure he will be warned against that one way or another," Detective Hawker agreed. "There were certain things the landlady said that made me wonder if Garth is even an Englishman. According to her he was extremely familiar with the continent. I came away with the idea we may be looking for a Frenchman."

"What about Patricia? Do you think she is alive?"

"That is a puzzle!"

"The old woman described her accurately," Ishbel said. "And she said that Patricia had been at the lodging as late as yesterday morning."

Detective Hawker asked, "Where can I get a likeness of this Patricia?"

"There are none here," she said. "My husband destroyed them all after her death."

"That was rather odd."

"He and she were not getting along well because he had discovered her unfaithfulness. He had a good reason for hating her."

"And perhaps even killing her?"

"I don't think he carried his hatred that far."

"Yet, it could be. The fall on the stairway has never been properly explained," the detective reminded her.

"If he tried to murder her and she recovered, why has she returned to him now?" Ishbel asked the stout detective.

He rubbed his chin. "The link could be opium. Your husband deals in it."

"I wish that were not a fact," she lamented. "It seems to make everything evil possible."

"Many are unhappy that our merchants, otherwise men of great respectability, are exporting the drug to China. I do not think it can continue."

She said, "There is one person who can give you a likeness of Patricia."

"Who?"

"Peter Graves, the artist I mentioned before. He lives only a few houses from here. He was once a suitor for her hand and in that period made many portraits of her."

Detective Hawker's round, ruddy face showed interest. "If I can find a suitable likeness, I can show it to the old woman and see whether she can identify it."

"That would be your next step," she suggested.

"Are you friendly with this Graves?"

"Yes."

"Is he liable to part with one of his smaller studies of the former Mrs. Davis?"

"I'm sure he'll find something to help you," she said.

"Then we should see him as soon as possible."

"I can take you over there now. We may find him at home. Being an artist, he keeps odd hours."

Detective Hawker said, "I would greatly appreciate it if you would let me meet him."

A few minutes later they were on the doorstep of Number Twenty-Eight. Ishbel used the rapper, and after a short wait the door was opened by the artist. He was still in his dressing robe, and he stared at Ishbel and her companion in surprise.

"Good morning," he said. "This is an early call."

"Please forgive us," Ishbel said, "but we need your help. This is Detective Hawker of the London Police."

"Do come in," Peter Graves invited them. "I'll be happy to help you in any way I can."

When they were in the living room Ishbel told the artist, "This concerns Patricia."

He raised his eyebrows. "Have you seen her again?"

"No. But others have," she said. "Or at least we think they have. We need some means of identifying her. And I suggested you might have a small sketch of her that you could give Detective Hawker."

"It would be a great help, sir," the stout detective said politely.

Peter hesitated. "Let me think! It should be small enough for you to carry easily in your pocket. I should have something. I made literally dozens of studies of her. Would a line drawing do?"

Detective Hawker said, "That would be excellent. Do you have such a drawing?"

"Wait a moment," the artist said, and he strode out of the room.

The detective turned to Ishbel and asked her, "Do you have Clara Sawyer's address?"

"No. But I think Mrs. Needles knows where she is working now."

"I should have had someone follow her last night, but I was too occupied with keeping track of you," the detective worried. "I want to question that girl. I'm sure she knows more than she has told you."

"Perhaps she has held off information, hoping to sell it to me later. She bargained for everything she gave me."

"That is quite possible," Hawker agreed.

Peter Graves came back into the room with a square of cardboard in his hand. He gave it to the detective and asked, "Will that do?"

Ishbel studied the neat pencil drawing of the unhappy beauty and said, "It is very good!"

Detective Hawker nodded. "This will be all I'll need. And you have my promise of its return when it has served its purpose."

"Thank you," Peter Graves said. "If anything happens to it, please don't worry. I have many other studies of Patricia, as Ishbel will tell you."

Ishbel said, "We do appreciate it."

Peter Graves asked them. "Just what is going on? How do the police come to be into this matter? I should have expected you to consult a spiritualist, Ishbel. I doubt if the police will be able to deal with a ghost."

Detective Hawker said earnestly, "I doubt if we could either. But are you so sure we are dealing with a ghost and not a living person?"

Peter Graves' handsome face showed a wry smile. "We have been asking ourselves that question lately. I'm afraid we have no practical answer."

"Nor have we," the stout detective said.

Ishbel said, "The sketch may help us. We are trying to identify a certain Reginald Garth and a girl whom he meets in the slums for opium sessions. The girl could be Patricia."

Peter frowned. "Then you still cling to your theory she is not really dead?"

"Yes," she said.

The artist shook his head in wonder. "I'll be stunned if you turn out to be right. Who is the man, this Reginald Garth?"

"No positive identification yet," Detective Hawker said. "And we may never succeed in discovering who he is. There is a chance he is a Frenchman."

"Probably in the country illegally," Peter observed. "I hear there are a lot of such people drifting across Europe."

"It makes the job of catching such a criminal most difficult," the detective agreed. "We will not take any more of your time, Mr. Graves. You have been most helpful."

Peter said, "Stay as long as you like. Ask me anything you think may help. I was once in love with Patricia. It is no secret and I'm not ashamed of it."

Ishbel turned to the detective and said, "Peter saw her occasionally almost up to the time of her death."

Hawker carefully placed the pencil sketch in his inside coat pocket and said, "May I ask, sir, if she ever spoke to you of having a male friend with a patch over one eye? A black patch over the left eye."

"I don't recall that she did," Peter said with a frown. "I know she was seeing someone. She told me that she had a lover and that Henry was furious about it. But she refused to tell me anything about him since she knew I also still could be jealous of her. Perhaps this lover of hers is the man with the black patch on his eye."

"Chances are he is," the detective said. "That is the description we have of this Reginald Garth. That he has a missing eye."

"Interesting," Peter Graves said. "It should provide you with a good clue. There aren't that many men wearing a black patch."

"More than you think," Ishbel said. "We have one here in Castle Square."

"We do?" Peter sounded surprised.

"Yes," she said. "Simpson."

"Your new gardener! Damme, you're right! You don't think your former fishmonger is the mystery man, do you?"

"No, sir," Detective Hawker said. "But it gives you an idea of how hard our job may be."

"I wish you luck," the artist said sincerely. And to Ishbel he added, "You will keep me advised as to what happens, won't you?"

"You may count on that," she told him.

When they had left the house Detective Hawker told her, "This may be our most important break in the case. Mr. Graves is a pleasant sort. Most obliging."

"I have always found him so," she said. And as they passed Number Twenty-Six, she added, "Lawyer Slade lives there. He knew Patricia well and visited her and Henry in the early days of their marriage. He is also a friend of Lord Carney, Patricia's father."

Detective Hawker showed interest. "I must have a chat with him."

"He is somewhat of an invalid. Suffers from the gout," she said.

"It has become a plague," the bow-legged Detective Hawker agreed.

When they reached the house, one of Hawker's men was there waiting for him. The two conferred for a few minutes in low voices, and then the detective sent the man on his way.

He afterwards turned to Ishbel and said, "We have caught your husband in a lie."

She bit her lip. "I'm not too surprised."

"He did not go to Liverpool."

"That doesn't startle me either. I suspected from the first that Liverpool was merely a pretence."

"He has remained in London, registered at the Westminster Hotel under the name of R. Garth!"

She had a hard time controlling her feelings. "Oh, no," she said faintly.

"He left a few hours ago. Perhaps he is at his office. I have an idea he might show up here before long to tell you of his visit to Liverpool."

Her head was reeling. "Then this means he is involved. Does it mean that he is the opium smoking Reginald Garth?"

"Nothing is certain at this point. But I ask you this: If he isn't playing the dual role of Garth, why would he register in a hotel under that name?"

"I don't know," she confessed.

"The name would have to be familiar to him. He couldn't hit on it by chance. So he knows the existence of Garth, even if he isn't Garth himself."

She sank into a chair near her and covered her face with her hands. Tears were brimming from her eyes, and she knew that even though she had feared the worst, she had gone on hoping that Henry would only be innocently involved. It no longer seemed likely.

After a little she touched her handkerchief to her eyes and asked, "What will you do now?"

"Try to find your husband, for a beginning. See that old woman and show her this portrait. Then make an attempt to learn whether we are dealing with a live Patricia or someone else."

"Who else?"

"I have no idea."

As he finished speaking, there was a commotion of voices in the rear hall. A moment later the elderly Mrs. Needles came hurrying down the dark passage towards them in what was clearly a state of near hysteria.

"Ma'am!" she cried and then began to sob.

Ishbel sprang to her feet and went to support the old woman, who appeared to be on the verge of fainting. "What is it?" she asked.

"It's shocking, ma'am!" Mrs. Needles sobbed. "There's been a body found! Out in the bushes behind the toolshed!"

"A body!" she exclaimed.

"Yes. Simpson found it just now," the old woman said and continued sobbing.

Ishbel turned to Detective Hawker and saw that the stout man was already on his way to the back door with surprising agility for one of his weight. She left the housekeeper to sob and hurried after the detective. Several of the other servants were clustered fearfully at the rear door, peeking out timorously. She pushed her way through them to follow Detective Hawker.

She found him and Simpson standing behind the toolshed staring down at a figure stretched out on the grass. It took only one glance at the purple, frightened face and the bulging eyes to tell her that this was Clara Sawyer, and that she'd been choked to death!

Detective Hawker saw her standing there and came to her. In a taut voice he said, "It is the Sawyer girl, isn't it?"

"Yes," she said in a near whisper.

"She knew too much," the detective said. "It wasn't wise of her to wander out here alone."

"She was using the side door to leave without being seen," she said.

"And she was seen by the wrong person," the detective replied grimly.

"What about Simpson?" she asked.

"I don't know," the stout man said. And he called out, "Simpson, come here."

The big man with the black patch over his eye left the body reluctantly, as if he was fascinated by it. He came lumbering over to them with a puzzled expression on his battered face. "I don't know why I didn't see her first thing when I went out this morning. I only found her a few minutes ago."

"Can you explain why you didn't notice the body before?" the detective asked.

"No, sir," Simpson said. "That's what bothers me. There is a heavy mist, and I didn't waste any time outside. I went straight into the shed."

Ishbel said, "The body was behind the hedge. You would have to go around the back of the shed to find it."

"I went to get a spade I left out there," the burly Simpson said. "And I almost turned and came back without noticing her. Then I saw her foot!"

Detective Hawker grunted. "Too bad I sent my man away. I'm going to need someone here. This body has to be watched. A doctor has to examine it and pronounce the means of death."

"She was choked," Ishbel said.

"I mean, we must have a proper medical report, even though we know what happened," the stout man said.

Simpson asked, "Should I stand guard on her for now?"

The detective considered. "Yes. I think that's a good idea. Don't let anyone near her."

"Aye, sir," Simpson said and went back to stand by the body.

Detective Hawker took Ishbel by the arm and said, "You go inside. It is cold and foggy out here. You'll get yourself a chill."

"Who could have done such a terrible thing?"

He led her towards the rear door. "Someone desperate to keep a secret. Perhaps the secret of a ghost!"

The frightened help were still clustered around the door. Detective Hawker at once ordered them to return to their work. They slowly went their various ways as the detective accompanied Ishbel out to the reception hall. Mrs. Needles was nowhere to be seen.

Ishbel gave the detective an anxious look. "Do you think there is a possibility Simpson did it?"

"He served a term for violence."

"That doesn't mean he has to be guilty now."

"I agree," the detective said. "In my opinion the person most likely to be guilty is the gentleman who calls himself Reginald Garth!"

Her eyes met his and she could not hide her horror. "You are saying my husband is the murderer!"

"Not exactly."

"But he did register in the hotel as R. Garth!"

"That weighs against him."

"But it's not enough to link him to this murder?"

"No," the stout detective said. "I'm afraid not. But I have an idea we can gradually put the pieces together until we are able to establish who the murderer is."

It was at this moment that the unexpected happened. The front door opened and Henry entered with his valise in hand. He looked at her and then at the detective with an expression of amazement crossing his handsome face.

He put down the valise and removed his top hat as he came forward to them. He said, "We seem to have a visitor, Ishbel."

She fought to keep the tremor from her voice as she said, "Yes. This is Detective Hawker of the London Police."

Henry frowned slightly. "The London police? I hope nothing too serious has happened, Detective Hawker. I have been away in Liverpool for a few days."

Chapter Eleven

Detective Hawker betrayed no expression at all as Henry offered this lie to them. He cleared his throat and said, "I'm glad to make your acquaintance, Mr. Davis. I believe you came by the station and made a complaint about your wife's being the victim of an attack."

"Yes," Henry said casually. "Some intruder made his way in and tried to throttle her."

"I was not at headquarters when you reported the crime," the stout man said, "but I was assigned to investigate it."

"Have you found the guilty party?" Henry asked.

"Not yet, sir."

Henry smiled coldly. "Then I suggest you remove yourself from the premises. I do not expect you to have a success. I warned my wife that before I even went to notify you."

"Henry, please!" she said, imploring him not to make it any worse for himself.

He gave her a disdainful glance. "Let me handle this, my dear. This is men's business."

Detective Hawker had a dangerous glint in his eyes. In his ponderous fashion he said, "Are you suggesting I close the files on this case?"

"That is exactly what I'm suggesting," Henry said.

There was a meaningful pause. Detective Hawker gave Ishbel a warning look. Then he addressed himself to her husband. "I'm sorry to tell you it won't be all that simple. I cannot close the case."

"Are you defying me?" Henry blustered.

"You could say that," the stout man said quietly.

"Then I shall talk with your superiors!" Henry said.

"You will have your chance to do that, sir."

"Don't think I won't take advantage of it," was Henry's warning. Ishbel had to fight herself to keep silent and refrain from telling him that he was in the deepest sort of trouble.

Detective Hawker fixed a stern glance on her husband as he said, "Someone was throttled in your garden last night, Mr. Davis."

Henry froze motionless and went pale. "I don't believe it!" he said in a shocked voice.

The stout detective went on, "A certain Miss Clara Sawyer, formerly in your employ. Do you recall her?"

Henry swallowed hard. "Yes, I do, actually. She was my first wife's personal maid. She left after my wife's tragic death."

Detective Hawker said, "Didn't you dismiss her, sir? Give her the sack?"

Henry looked nervously at Ishbel and then at the stout man. "You're probably right! I'd forgotten about that. Yes, I believe I did suggest she leave."

Detective Hawker cleared his throat again. "About your visit to Liverpool, sir. The police know that you did not leave the city."

"That's a monstrous lie!" Henry blustered, but he was much more on the defensive now.

Ishbel could keep silent no longer. She blurted out, "They know, Henry. It is useless for you to lie!"

He came to her in a dazed fashion and placed an arm around her as he asked, "What kind of plot is this against me?"

"No plot against you, sir," the detective said. "It would seem to me that the plotting is of your making. We know you were at the Westminster Hotel and that you were registered under the name of R. Garth!"

Henry listened in a despairing way and then said, "All right. Suppose I was in London. I had good reason to be here: a personal matter which I had to attend to."

"What personal matter, sir?" Detective Hawker asked.

"I don't think I have to answer that!" Henry protested.

"Would it be to meet your first wife in a hovel down in the East End?"

"What nonsense are you talking?" Henry demanded. "My first wife is dead!"

Detective Hawker went on in his stolid way, "Is she, sir? Strange that a number of people claim to have seen her."

"This is all madness!" Henry raged. He turned to Ishbel. "What do I have to do to end this questioning and get this fellow out of the house?"

"Tell him the truth, Henry," she advised him in a low voice.

"The truth?" Henry echoed. "I refuse to discuss any more of my private affairs with you, Detective Hawker."

"That is too bad, sir," the detective said. "This Miss Sawyer sold your wife information to the effect that your first wife regularly met a man named Reginald Garth in an East End hovel. She said that your first wife and this fellow met for the purpose of smoking opium together. And now we find that you registered at the hotel as R. Garth. Can you explain this?"

Henry removed his arm from around Ishbel and directed a show of rage at the stout detective. "I will not attempt to discuss any of this. My former wife Patricia is dead. Whatever she may have done is no longer important, and neither is the identity of Reginald Garth!"

"You registered at the hotel as R. Garth, sir. Are you Reginald Garth?"

"No. You'd be utterly mad to think I was."

"Then why did you use that name?"

"It just came to me!"

"Come now, sir," the detective said. "You can't expect us to believe that!"

Henry turned to Ishbel imploringly. "I tell you I am innocent. I've done nothing wrong!"

She said, "Why did you lie about being in Liverpool?"

"I had good reason. Personal reasons I can't explain."

"Not even to your wife?" she said.

"It doesn't concern you! You are only a part of my life! The best part to be sure, but I cannot open the door to all that I do or have done!"

Ishbel said, "You don't seem to understand. You cannot account for your actions. A murder has been committed here. You have used the name of the man with the strongest motive for the murder."

A trapped look crossed her husband's handsome face. He said, "I'm actually suspected of murder?"

"I'm afraid so, sir," Detective Hawker said. "Your wife couldn't have put it more clearly."

"This is absurd!" Henry said in weak protest.

"That may be, sir," the stout detective said. "But because of the strong circumstantial guilt against you I will have to hold you as the suspected slayer of the woman, Sawyer."

Henry turned to her. "Ishbel! You don't believe any of this?"

"I don't want to," she said.

"Get Timothy Slade," he ordered her.

She hesitated. "I don't think he can come here. He is ill with the gout."

Henry said, "Tell him the circumstances. He will come."

Detective Hawker asked, "Who is Timothy Slade?"

"Henry's lawyer," she said. "I mentioned him to you. He lives next door."

The detective said, "If your husband wishes to consult legal counsel I will not stop him. But I also ask that you send a messenger to the police station. Ask them to send me help; let them know there has been a murder here."

"Very well," she said. "I'll go speak to Lawyer Slade myself, and I'll have Mrs. Needles send one of the maids to the police station."

She left her husband and the old detective standing facing each other grimly in the reception hall while she went out to the kitchen and recruited Mrs. Needles. The old woman was still in a dreadful state, but Ishbel managed to get the message through to her. A maid would go to the police.

Ishbel found the old lawyer on the second floor of his home with his gout-ridden leg stretched out as usual on a footstool. Breathlessly she told him, "Henry is in trouble, Lawyer Slade! He has asked for you!"

The old man sat up and resting one hand on his cane asked her, "What is it now?"

She quickly told him, ending with, "He is waiting for you. Detective Hawker threatens to take him in charge for murder!"

Lawyer Slade gingerly let his bad foot down on the floor. It was encased in a large slipper. He wheezed, "Help me up! But be easy!"

She gave him support on his bad side, and he reached a tottering standing position. He stood there for a moment with his lips compressed. "Stay by me," he said. "I think I can make it with your help."

Their progress was slow and extremely painful for the old man. But at last she helped him up to the entrance at Twenty-Two, where he stood leaning heavily on her arm. She opened the door and they went inside. Henry was seated in a chair in a despairing attitude. As soon as the old lawyer hobbled in, he rose to greet him.

"Slade, you must tell this fellow he's mad!" Henry exclaimed. "He wants to arrest me for the murder of a girl I haven't seen in months."

Timothy Slade nodded grimly. "I have heard about it from Ishbel. You must be reasonable. Why did you say you were going to Liverpool? And why did you register in a hotel here under the name of R. Garth?"

Henry hesitated for a long moment. Then he lifted his hands in a gesture of resignation. "I can't tell you!"

Lawyer Timothy Slade warned him, "Unless you come out with the truth, you are in a bad position."

"You mean I can be held?" Henry said.

Detective Hawker spoke up. "Your lawyer knows that. I'll give you a final chance. Will you explain who R. Garth is and why you registered under his name?"

"No!" Henry said firmly.

Detective Hawker said. "What about Patricia?"

"She's dead!" Henry replied.

Detective Hawker said, "Then you were seen with a ghost?"

Lawyer Slade now turned to Henry and said, "I saw her here in the court one night, Henry. Is she alive?"

Henry gave a deep sigh. Then he said, "All right! Enough questions! Arrest me if you will! I have nothing more to say."

Timothy Slade eyed him sternly. "Do you realize you are sealing your own fate?"

"It seems you all think me a murderer," Henry said. "What is the point of trying to dissuade you?"

Ishbel stepped forward to him. "I don't think you killed that girl, but I'm sure you must be protecting whoever did do it. Who is Reginald Garth?"

Henry shrugged. "I can't answer that."

Detective Hawker said, "I have no choice. I must take Mr. Davis in. Perhaps after he is in custody a while he will choose to talk."

So the issue was decided. A few minutes later a carriage came with several other members of the police. Shortly after that a doctor arrived to make the official examination of the murdered Clara Sawyer. His finding was as had been expected: the girl had been throttled.

Detective Hawker took a silent and embittered Henry off in the same carriage. One bobby was left in charge of the house, while the others accompanied the body of the girl to police headquarters.

Ishbel was left with only old Lawyer Slade to comfort her. Henry had kissed her with great tenderness before he was taken away. It seemed as if he felt they would not meet again.

Tearfully she asked the old lawyer, "What are we to do now?"

Timothy Slade was sitting in an easy chair with his bad foot outstretched. He said, "The game isn't over yet, not by any means. They will hold Henry for a while and question him, but I doubt that they can truly charge him with the murder on the evidence so far presented."

"But if he is the mysterious Reginald Garth?"

"I have to think about that," Lawyer Slade said. "If you will help me back to my place, I will write a note to my junior partner and have him take an active role on behalf of Henry at once. I'm sure we'll be able to manage something."

Ishbel called Simpson, who was able to give the old man more aid than she could have managed. It seemed to her significant that Detective Hawker had shown no sign of suspecting Simpson of involvement in the murder.

Hardly had Simpson and the old man left when another carriage rolled up. This time it was her cousin Ernest come to see her.

She greeted him warmly. "I have never wanted to see you more," she said. And she told him all that had happened.

Ernest looked shocked. "Henry has actually been arrested?"

"As good as," she said.

"And that girl was murdered before she ever got away from here?"

"Yes."

"Someone wanted to shut her up."

"I know," Ishbel agreed. "But I don't want to think it was Henry."

Ernest said, "I came to take you in to the bank. Uncle Walter and Dr. Gregory are there waiting to see you."

"I'm in no fit state," she protested.

"There's nothing you can do here," the young man said. "Uncle Walter has his own private office. We can talk freely there. He has a great deal of influence. I think you should come with me and try to get their help."

She realized his arguments were sound. "You honestly feel that is what I should do?"

"Yes."

"Very well," she said. "Give me a few minutes to get ready."

The London streets were crowded with traffic at this late morning period. Horse-coaches, drays, private carriages and country wagons with produce all battled for passage in the narrow thoroughfares. There were endless stops, much shouting and cursing on the part of the drivers, and extremely slow progress.

"We could have walked almost as quickly," she complained.

"I'd say we are past the worst bottlenecks now," Ernest said. "London is far worse than Edinburgh when it comes to traffic."

"I wonder where Henry is being held," she worried. "I ought to visit him."

"Lawyer Slade will get all that information for you," her cousin said.

Finally the carriage drew up before the majestic, columned front of the famous English bank with which the House of Stewart was associated. Ernest helped Ishbel out onto the busy pavement and guided her into the bank.

The private office her Uncle Walter was using was reached through a door and hallway on the right. Ernest led her to the office and knocked respectfully. After a moment the door was opened by her Uncle Walter.

The stern, tall Walter Stewart had lost none of his erectness with age. He was still an imposing figure. He reached out to take her in his arms, saying, "My dear Ishbel, I'm very sorry for all this trouble you're having."

The sound of his Scots burr and his tone of sympathy brought tears to her eyes. She clung to him. "Oh, Uncle Walter!"

The stern man patted her gently and said, "It cannot be that bad. Get a hold on yourself like a true Scots lass and come greet Dr. Gregory. He has been wanting to see you."

She allowed herself to be led into the large, richly decorated office to the spot where the little doctor was waiting. The old man showed a smile on his thin face beneath the brown wig. He took her hands in his.

"Your mother and father send their warm wishes," Dr. Jock Gregory said, "and the children are well and happy."

"Thank you, Dr. Gregory," she said.

The venerable Dr. Gregory led her to a chair by the broad

mahogany desk that dominated the room. He said, "Now you must sit down, calm yourself, and tell us all about it."

Uncle Walter seated himself behind the desk and told her, "We want to hear everything."

Standing a little behind her, Ernest informed the two older men, "There has been a new development. Ishbel's husband has been taken into custody by the police."

Little Jock Gregory showed concern. "So it has come to that!"

Uncle Walter Stewart said, "Regardless of this development, I want to hear it all from the start."

Feeling as if she were in a kind of trance, Ishbel recited it all for them. She ended with, "In spite of everything, I love my husband and I hope he is not guilty."

Uncle Walter, looking more stern than ever, drummed the fingers of his right hand on the desk top. He finally said, "The important questions seem to be: What has your husband been up to in these various secret activities? Who is Reginald Garth, and where is he? And is Patricia alive or dead?"

Dr. Jock Gregory spoke up. "You say that Patricia was a daughter of Lord Carney?"

"Yes," Ishbel said.

The old doctor turned to Walter Stewart and said, "By a stroke of good fortune I happen to be a friend of Sir William Perkins, who has been family doctor to Lord Carney for many years."

Walter Stewart said, "Then perhaps you can contact him and find out if Patricia was alive when her father took possession of her."

Dr. Jock Gregory nodded. "It will be strictly between us as professional men. I do not know that I can allow you to quote my findings directly. But if Perkins will confide in me, we will at least know the truth about Patricia."

Ishbel was encouraged by even this small hope of finding some basic facts. "If you only can find out!"

"I promise you I shall do my best," the old doctor said.

Uncle Walter told her, "I know some people with influence here in the city. I'll see what I can do on your husband's behalf. Of course, should he be proven guilty, there is little that can be done."

"I understand," she said. "I appreciate what you are trying to do for me. It is good to be close to the family again."

"Perhaps after all this you may return to Edinburgh," her Uncle Walter said. "Stormhaven is very empty these days. I would be glad to have you and your children come and live with us."

"How is Aunt Heather?" she asked.

"Not well," her Uncle said soberly. "She rarely gets out of bed these days."

"I'm going to discuss her case with some London specialists who are friends of mine," Dr. Jock Gregory said. "I have not given up hope for her."

"Amen to that!" Walter Stewart said, a gentleness showing on his stern face.

"And my father?" she asked the thin old doctor.

"He is better," Dr. Gregory said with a small smile. "He was on his feet and talking about taking back part of his practice again when I left."

"That is good news," she said.

The little doctor stood up and consulted his pocket watch. "I must get along. At this time of day Sir William Perkins usually takes luncheon at a club to which we both belong. With luck I can catch him there."

Walter Stewart also rose and said, "And you and Ernest shall have lunch with me, Ishbel."

"I'm not hungry," she protested.

"We'll have none of that nonsense," Uncle Walter said with a hint of his usual sternness. "Only saints are the better for fasting. You will be better off with some good food in your stomach."

He was not a man one could easily argue with, and so within a half-hour Ishbel found herself at a table in one of London's finest restaurants with her Uncle Walter on one side of her and Cousin Ernest on the other.

After they had ordered, she said, "I don't know what I shall do if Henry is disgraced. I'm so ashamed for bringing this on the family."

Walter Stewart smiled in his cold fashion. "The Stewarts have known scandal before and recovered from it."

Ernest said, "You are thinking of Great Aunt Peggy?"

His uncle nodded. "Yes. She was the mistress of the highwayman Black Charlie. And her illegitimate son Billy was raised as one of the family."

Ishbel said, "Didn't he join the navy?"

"Yes," Walter Stewart said. "When he was a mere lad. He was killed in a naval action just after his twenty-third birthday."

"How sad!" she said.

Ernest asked their uncle, "What sort of person was he? Did he mind that he was illegitimate and the son of a highwayman?"

"Perhaps it bothered him," Walter Stewart said. "He was a quiet lad, kept a good deal to himself. And as soon as he could, he left the family and entered the navy."

Ernest said, "My father has a theory that Billy felt he could lose himself in the service. That he would not be known and could be accepted without the stigma of his father shadowing him."

"That may well be," Walter Stewart said. "Roger was

closer to Billy than the rest of us. Perhaps they talked about this. I know your father was very upset when we received word of Billy's death."

"He still speaks well of him," Ernest said.

Uncle Walter smiled at her again. "So you must not worry. Whatever comes of this, the Stewarts stand by their own in a crisis. And few dare to point a finger at us."

She was heartened by her uncle's words, though she knew that she would go through a period of bleak despair if Henry proved to be a murderer. There was hope for her children. The family would see that they did not suffer. They could grow up in Edinburgh and not know the truth about their father until they were old enough to cope with it.

The luncheon was an excellent one. Afterwards Ernest saw her to a cab. Uncle Walter promised to be in touch with her as soon as he or Dr. Gregory found out anything of significance. She rode back to Number Twenty-Two in a slightly better frame of mind than when she left. But when she entered Castle Square and saw two other carriages waiting at the door, she felt herself go taut once more. Something must have happened.

The driver helped her from the carriage, and she hurried across the sidewalk and up the steps into the house. When she opened the door, she was confronted by Detective Hawker, who had been conferring with a uniformed bobby. The bobby stood back respectfully so that the stout detective could give his full attention to Ishbel.

She exclaimed, "Have you set my husband free?"

Detective Hawker shook his head. "No, Mrs. Davis."

"Then why are you here?"

"I regret to inform you that your husband escaped on his way to the police station."

"Escaped!"

"Yes. I must admit to some negligence in the matter. You see, he was so completely resigned, I was not expecting this sort of thing on his part."

"How did he manage it?"

"We were caught in a traffic jam," the detective said. "I leaned out the window to give the driver some directions, and at the same instant your husband swung the opposite door of the carriage open and dashed off through the clutter of vehicles!"

Ishbel felt it was the worst possible thing that could have happened—a confirmation of his guilt. She said, "You weren't able to catch him?"

The stout detective eyed her ruefully. "I am not ideally equipped for chasing after a fugitive in a street crowded with traffic. I was no match for him, ma'am."

"So what now?" she asked in despair.

"I returned here to let you know, on the chance he might head back here."

"That is not likely," she said. "He is more apt to go to that hovel by the East End docks."

"Neither he nor the woman will dare show up there now," Detective Hawker said. "I have men posted all around the courtyard."

She said, "I don't know what to think."

"Nor do I," the stout man said. "I confess it."

She said, "I had luncheon with my uncle and a doctor friend of the family. They are going to do all they can to help."

Detective Hawker said, "I will have to keep men here, but I will place them inconspicuously."

"What about Simpson?" she said. "You have not mentioned him in all this."

"No," he said, "because I now am at the point of agreeing with you that he is not guilty of any offense."

"I'm glad," she said.

217

"There is a good deal of mystery about the man," the detective said. "He is reluctant to talk about his past."

"Most ex-convicts must be the same in that regard," she suggested.

"He refuses to talk about his life before he was in prison."

"He served in the navy. He told me that."

"But he is vague about it," Detective Hawker complained. "He has mentioned neither the place where he was wounded or the officer he served under. He will not tell me anything."

"Is it important that you should know?"

"I like to know everything possible about anyone even loosely associated with a case."

"Maybe I can get him to talk," she suggested. "I have always been able to have a good relationship with him."

"You could try," Detective Hawker agreed.

"What else can I do?" she asked.

"Remain here and behave as if nothing were wrong."

"That will not be easy," she said.

"I'm sure you can do it," Detective Hawker told her. "We will keep on the lookout for your husband and that mystery woman."

"The ghostly Patricia," she said bitterly.

"She may not be so ghostly," Detective Hawker said. "I'm getting some ideas about her."

He remained for a few minutes and then left in one of the carriages. Two bobbies stayed to guard the house, one on the outside in the garden and the other in the house in the reception hall.

Ishbel went out into the garden to see if she could find Simpson. The fog had lifted and the sun was wanly shining through dull clouds. She stopped by the toolshed, but he wasn't there, nor was he anywhere in sight in the garden.

She went inside and asked Mrs. Needles, "Have you seen Simpson?"

The old woman was red-eyed from weeping and in a generally upset state. "After all that has happened this morning, I haven't even thought of him!"

Ishbel said, "Will you have his room checked and see if he's there?"

"I will," the housekeeper promised. She vanished to return a few minutes later with the news, "He isn't there, ma'am."

Ishbel was concerned. "Then he must have left. I would have expected the police to stop him if they saw him leaving."

"With all the confusion, he wouldn't have much trouble getting away," was Mrs. Needles' opinion. And it turned out she was right. The house and grounds were searched, but apparently Simpson had vanished.

As the day wore on, Ishbel grew continually more nervous. She was on edge from expecting Henry to appear at any minute and have to confront the waiting police. But he did not come. Nor was there word from anyone else.

Around six o'clock a carriage pulled up in front of Number Twenty-Two, and little Dr. Jock Gregory alighted from it in a sprightly manner for someone of his age.

Ishbel was at the door to let him in. "I'm so glad to see you," she said. "Henry escaped from the police, and I've been here waiting for him to arrive."

Dr. Gregory surprised her by saying, "I know all about it. I have talked with Detective Hawker."

"Did you find anything out about Patricia?" she asked.

"I saw Sir William Perkins," the little man said with an air of mystery.

"And what did he say?"

"Patricia is definitely dead."

"Henry has always insisted upon that. Then who was it we have seen? I saw her, and so did several others. The landlady of that wretched hovel identified her from Peter Graves' drawing of her."

Dr. Jock Gregory gave her a knowing glance. "So the unfaithful wife has become a loving ghost! A ghost whom I predict you will see soon again!"

"I don't understand," she said.

"I do not expect you to," the old man said. "Will you allow me to spend the night here?"

"If you like."

"I do not think you should be alone," he said.

"I'm sure Detective Hawker will have one or two of his bobbies here," she said.

"That is hardly family comfort," Dr. Gregory said with a concerned look on his thin face. "You need someone you can talk with."

Ishbel knew he was right. The strain of waiting alone had been great. Now that the sprightly little man was on hand to divert her with his conversation, it helped a great deal.

At dinner he told her, "Your son William is a keen lad. He tells me that he wants to be a doctor like his grandfather."

"I know," she agreed. "He has talked of nothing else since he has been able to understand what being a doctor means."

The old man with the brown wig chuckled. "Encourage him," he said. "I say it is just as important for Stewarts to be doctors as to be bankers."

Her lovely face shadowed. "His father approved of his interest. I shudder to think how the children will be hurt if Henry cannot be cleared of this."

"I thought you had faith in Henry."

"I did until today. When he refused to answer the questions the police put to him and then ran off, I found even my faith faltering."

Dr. Gregory said, "Still, he may have had some good reason for behaving as he did."

"I can't think of any."

"And he must still be at large or you would have been informed by the police."

"Detective Hawker promised to let me know the moment there were any developments."

"I should say he is dependable. He will keep his word."

Ishbel lamented, "And now Simpson has vanished as well."

"I didn't meet him, did I?" Dr. Gregory asked.

"No," she said. "He is an ex-sailor whom I hired as our gardener. He has done very well, despite the fact he has a rather villainous look. He wears a black eye patch to cover a missing eye."

"So he matches the description of the mysterious Reginald Garth," the old doctor commented. "You mentioned that he also wore an eye patch."

"That is true but seems to be merely coincidence," she said. "I don't attach any importance to it."

"You're probably right," the veteran doctor said, "but I should like to meet this Simpson."

"If he returns, I'll see that you do," she promised.

"I must retire early," he said, "but my bedroom is just across the hall from yours. If you need me for anything in the night, don't hesitate to call me."

She again thanked him for his kindness in remaining with her. Then he turned to go up to bed. In the hallway they met Chen. The old Chinese was more subdued than usual and seemed anxious to avoid speaking to them. He went by them with head bowed.

Dr. Jock Gregory stopped and said, "I didn't know you had a Chinese in your employ."

"Henry's father brought him here, and he is very loyal to Henry."

"I would expect that," the doctor agreed. "These people are generally very devoted. Has Detective Hawker questioned him?"

"Not extensively."

"It might be a good idea," the spry old doctor said. "He may know more of Henry's whereabouts than you'd guess."

"I'll speak to Detective Hawker when he returns," she promised.

Ishbel stayed up only a little while after the veteran doctor. During this time she thought about Chen and wondered if the old doctor might be right. Henry might have confided certain matters to his Chinese servant that he did not venture to discuss with her. One policeman was still stationed in the front hall and another in the garden when she went up to bed.

As she prepared for bed, she again experienced a feeling of dread. Her fears pressed in on her, and she went to the drawer where she kept the pistol that had turned up so providentially. Even with the police in the house, she felt she might need it.

Reaching beneath the blankets in the lower drawer where she kept the pistol hidden, she was startled to find—nothing. She rummaged frantically for it, but there was no use. The pistol had vanished in the same way it had appeared!

Chapter Twelve

The eerie feeling of danger that had crept over her earlier now became more powerful. Ishbel closed the dresser drawer with an expression of awe on her attractive face. She had nothing to help her in this moment of terror. All she could do if she was attacked was to call out and trust that some of the others might hear her.

Still dogged by her fears, she got into bed and blew out the remaining candle flame, leaving the room in darkness. She lay back on the pillow and tried to determine why she had suddenly been struck by this sense of being menaced. Fear had become her almost constant companion in the old house, but this was something rather different.

She knew there was at least one policeman in the house and another on the grounds, but the terror that stalked her might not be of a nature with which the police could cope. It seemed to her there was a supernatural horror about this new threat.

Somewhere in the darkness her husband was hiding from the police. Detective Hawker, who was usually right, felt that Henry might attempt to return to Number Twenty-Two in the night. If he did come, the police would be waiting for him. She winced at the thought that the man she loved might be both an opium addict and a murderer!

He had taken the name of Reginald Garth without being able to give any satisfactory reason for it. He had claimed to be in Liverpool when all the time he had been registered in London under a false name. These things counted against him.

The fear-distorted face of the throttled Clara Sawyer

haunted Ishbel. The former personal maid of Patricia's had obviously been murdered because she knew too much. And once she had begun to sell her knowledge, bit by bit, the killer had been forced to silence her.

Ishbel felt some guilt in the unfortunate girl's death. She had tempted the former maid to sell the information, all the while knowing that it would put her in danger. At the time Ishbel had hoped to use the information to help capture the murderer, but it had not worked out that way.

Eventually Ishbel's eyes closed and she began to sleep lightly. She had no idea how long she slept before she was wakened by the sound of a door creaking open. She quickly sat up. Staring into the darkness, she saw the lovely phantom face of Patricia gazing at her from the foot of the bed!

She was so frozen with terror she could neither cry out nor move. The phantom stood there for a moment with a look of infinite sadness on the beautiful face. Then she turned and walked out through the open door into the dark hallway.

Ishbel threw back the bedclothes and, without even slowing to put on her slippers, hurried across the room to follow the phantom figure. When she reached the hallway, she saw the black-cloaked Patricia moving across the landing on her way to the stairs. At the same instant another figure came down the stairs above and made directly for the woman in the cloak!

Ishbel caught a glance of the face of the second figure and saw that it was a fairly young man wearing a black eye patch. It had to be the mysterious Reginald Garth! He raised his hand, and she saw the glitter of a knife in it by the glow of the single night lamp bracketed on the wall. The man plunged the knife into the girl's back. Ishbel finally found her voice. She screamed out as the girl slumped to the floor of the landing.

The killer gave Ishbel a startled glance and seemed about to pursue her. Then, thinking better of it, he plunged back up the dark stairway which led to the floor above—a floor used mostly for storage.

The first person to appear in response to Ishbel's scream was old Dr. Gregory, a dressing gown thrown hurriedly over his nightgown. He came to her and asked, "What is it?"

"Look!" She pointed to the figure on the floor of the landing with a growing pool of blood around it.

"I knew it!" the old doctor cried and ran forward to give what attention he could to the stabbed woman.

Now bedlam broke forth in the ancient building. The police and the servants came crowding on the scene at almost the same moment. Ishbel and the venerable doctor had to plead with them to stand back and use their energy to try to locate the killer who had fled.

Dr. Gregory was kneeling by the girl and had her head propped up in his arms. He told Ishbel, "Her life is draining away. She can't last more than a few minutes. Did you have a quarrel with her?"

"No," Ishbel protested. "She came into my room and I woke up, and when she went out, I decided to follow her. I reached the hallway just in time to see the man with the black eye patch stab her and flee."

"Was it Simpson?" the old doctor asked.

"No. Someone younger. I didn't get a good look at him. But I saw the eye patch."

The doctor told the two bobbies, "She says he went up the stairs. Take a look up there—but there's no certainty he's still there! Check the roof and the roofs of the houses adjoining!"

Old Mrs. Needles in her dressing gown pushed forward to look at the pale, lovely face of the stabbed woman. She gasped and declared, "It's Mrs. Patricia, back from the dead!"

"Not quite," Dr. Jock Gregory said.

"Has she a chance?" Ishbel asked.

The little doctor shook his head. "I can no longer feel her pulse. She's dead now."

The door below burst open and stout Detective Hawker came rushing in and up the stairs. He said, "I was outside when she came to the Square and went around to the back of the house to get in! What's happened to her?"

Ishbel said, "Reginald Garth stabbed her. I saw him do it from down the hall."

The stout man gave her a disappointed glance. "And you didn't sound the alarm?"

"I cried out, but it was too late!"

"Where are my men?" the stout man wanted to know.

"Upstairs looking for the killer," Dr. Jock Gregory said. "He fled up there!"

"They'd better get him," the detective said grimly. Then he turned his attention to Mrs. Needles and the other servants. He ordered them, "Back to your rooms, all of you! You're in the way! We don't want any of you hurt!"

With some murmurings they reluctantly left the landing. The doctor was still bending over the stabbed woman. He looked up and informed Detective Hawker. "It's no good! She's dead!"

"Blast it!" the stout man exclaimed. "We've lost out again!"

"Not if your men catch him," Dr. Gregory said. "Let us take her body into one of the empty bedrooms and cover it decently until your medical examiner gets here."

"Very well," Detective Hawker said, and he took the feet of the dead woman while the thin, little doctor gamely lifted her head and shoulders. Together they carried her into the nearest empty bedroom.

Ishbel found a blanket and dropped it over the pool of blood that had formed on the landing floor. She was leaning against the banister feeling she was near fainting when the two men came out.

She asked, "Was it Patricia?"

"No," Dr. Gregory said. "Patricia's half-sister!"

"Half-sister," she gasped. "I have always understood Lord Carney had only one daughter."

Dr. Gregory looked grim. "That was what everyone thought. But Carney had an illegitimate daughter, Lorna, by a French woman. Until a few years ago, when her mother died, this girl lived in Paris. She returned shortly before the death of Patricia."

"She was the image of Patricia," Ishbel said.

The old doctor nodded. "I have never seen two young women who so resembled each other. They could have been twins, though they had different mothers."

"You found all this out from Sir William Perkins?" she said.

"And more!" Detective Hawker grumbled. "But it won't do any good if they don't catch that Garth!" And he left them to lumber up the dark stairs to the upper story and the roof to see what was happening in the pursuit of the killer.

Ishbel said, "What was she doing here?"

"Blackmail and dope, a little of both," Dr. Gregory said.

"Go on," she urged him.

"According to Sir William Perkins, his patient, Lord Carney, has been systematically blackmailed for nearly ten years. It began when this Garth met Lorna on the continent and from her mother learned who she was. He initiated the girl in drugs and a good deal more. By the time she returned to England with him she was his slave. He first had her go to Patricia and get the blackmail money from her and drugs from Henry. At least that is what we think."

"And one of them killed Patricia?"

"It is likely there was some sort of quarrel, during which Patricia was shoved down the stairs to her death. The fact that Henry did not expose these two and their wicked game tends to make me think that Henry may actually be Garth. After all, we know he registered at the Westminster Hotel under that name in order to meet the girl and give her blackmail and drugs."

She said, "You think Henry may be the man they're trying to capture up there?"

"It may be. I hope not."

"How was this Lorna able to blackmail Patricia and Lord Carney?" she asked.

"Lord Carney had become fanatically religious. He could not bear the thought that his illegitimate child might be brought to light. Nor was he proud that this neglected girl had become a drug addict. He wanted to keep it all a secret. Of course he blamed himself when Patricia was killed in that mysterious accident. But he could not reveal what he suspected."

Hopefully, Ishbel said, "Perhaps Henry is not Garth after all. Perhaps he has done nothing worse than conspire to keep the silence about this Lorna. When Patricia was killed, he may have become the go-between for the blackmailers with Lord Carney."

"That is possible."

"That could explain the mysterious visits, the smell of opium in his study after Lorna was here. It may be why he tried to meet them and silence them after Clara Sawyer's murder. He could not talk without betraying Lord Carney's secret, and then it would all have been for nothing."

Dr. Gregory said, "I hope you are right—that your Henry was nothing more than an unwilling agent. But that leaves us with no Garth. And we know a Garth exists. He was the evil power behind Lorna. What about Garth?"

"I don't know," she said unhappily. She tried to recall the face she had glimpsed so briefly and decide whether it could have been her husband wearing a black eye patch. It was all a blur to her.

"Don't pretend if you know," the old doctor warned her. "If Henry is Garth, you know he is a dangerous man—a threat to us all."

"I can't say!"

"You told us you saw the killer for a moment. Was he masked?"

"No!"

"And you saw the black eye patch! What about his face? Surely you saw enough of his face to recognize him?"

"No!" she wailed.

"I'm sorry," Dr. Gregory said and placed a comforting arm around her as she wept.

There was the sound of voices from above. A moment later a disgruntled Detective Hawker and his two bobbies came down the steps. The stout man removed his hat and mopped his perspiring brow.

"We lost him!" he said with disgust. "I knew we would! He's a sly one!"

"How could he have escaped?" the doctor asked.

"Just as you guessed, over the rooftops. We lost him completely. All the houses in the half-circle are joined. It was a hopeless task."

"What now?"

"He'll have to find his way back to the street at some

229

point," Hawker reasoned. "We'll go outside and keep a sharp look. In the meantime I'll report the murder to the station and send for more men! We'll stay here until dawn if we have to!"

"I've explained everything to Ishbel—" the doctor said "—all we found out about Lorna."

Detective Hawker came up to her, his ruddy face still damp with perspiration. He said, "You saw the killing! Was it your husband?"

"I don't think so," she faltered.

"You should know!" the detective snapped.

"I couldn't tell. The light isn't very good, and it all took place in a matter of seconds!" she told him.

His round face was grim. "I hope you haven't started to lie to us!"

"No!" she protested.

The detective said, "I'll leave her in your care, Doctor. I'll go down below and join my men. But I'll be back shortly!"

"I'll look after her," the old doctor promised.

Ishbel waited until the detective had gone downstairs. Then she turned to the old doctor and said, "I feel ill. I must go back to bed."

"That is wise," he agreed. "I'll see you to your room."

"I'll be all right," she said.

"Just the same, I'd prefer to accompany you into the bedroom," the old man insisted. "Let us take no chances."

She allowed him to escort her back into the room. He found matches and lighted the candle on the bedside table. He told her, "Let the candle burn. Don't leave yourself in total darkness. And if you hear anything, don't hesitate to call to me. I'll leave my door open."

She said, "There was a pistol in the dresser. When I went to find it tonight, it wasn't there."

"Who gave you the pistol? Henry?"

"No. I simply found it there one night."

"And you never found out who put it there?"

"I didn't dare ask. But I kept it under my pillow, and the night Lorna came into the room first, I fired at her. I missed, of course, but it scared them off."

Dr. Jock Gregory's thin face showed thought. "But when you looked for it tonight, the weapon had vanished?"

"As if removed by a ghostly hand."

He turned to the dresser. "Which drawer was it in?"

"The lower one. It was hidden under the blankets. I counted on having it tonight. When I looked for it and didn't find it, I was frantic!"

The old man went over, opened the dresser drawer and felt under the blankets. It was only a moment before he turned to her with a questioning look on his face and held out the pistol for her to see.

"It was there!" he said.

Her eyes widened. "Not when I looked for it earlier."

"It was caught within the folds of the second blanket," the doctor said. "That was how you came to miss it." He examined it. "It seems to be loaded. Do you want to keep it?"

"Yes. I'd feel much safer with it."

"You know how to use it? I don't want you injuring yourself."

"I used it before," she said, taking the pistol. "I can handle it."

"Good luck, then," Dr. Gregory said. And he went out and closed the door after him.

Ishbel felt a little more secure with the weapon in her possession again. She knew she couldn't sleep, but she went back to bed and sat propped against the pillows with the pistol in her hands.

231

The old house seemed full of phantom sounds. And there were voices from outside which belonged to humans. She could hear them in a muffled sort of way as Detective Hawker and his men conducted their search for the murderer.

What a place of violence the quiet house had become! Two murders within a period of days and Patricia surely a murder victim earlier—all because the venal old Lord Carney had been determined to cover his past sins. Had he not catered to the blackmailers, none of this would have happened.

Now his dark secret was sure to be brought out in the open. What a scandal it would create in high London circles! Henry had been dragged into it and destroyed by it. Ishbel could not believe he was anything but a victim. She did not see him in the role of the murderous Garth.

Perhaps before the night was over, Garth would be captured by Detective Hawker and his bobbies and the truth would come out. In the meanwhile she must wait, with her nerves becoming more tense every minute. Never had a night seemed so long to her! No wonder Henry had changed so and become so haggard. He had taken on all the dealings with the infamous two for ailing old Lord Carney.

She was so lost in these speculations that at first she did not notice as the closet door near the head of her bed opened a crack. It was only when it opened a bit more that she was alerted into action. She turned quickly with the pistol in her hand.

"Wait!" The plea came in an anxious whisper.

"I have you covered," she warned.

"Don't shoot! It's Henry!"

"Henry!" she gasped, lowering the gun a little.

The door opened and Henry stepped out—a haggard, disheveled Henry who looked years older than the man she had last seen leaving with the police.

He whispered, "I won't harm you!"

"Don't come any closer," she told him. "I know how to use this!"

"Why do you want to shoot me?"

"Because you must be Garth! Why else would you be hiding here? How did you manage to get back?"

"I'm not Garth and I didn't manage to get back," Henry whispered. "I came up the back stairway after you discovered Lorna dead on the landing. I hid in here because I felt I could count on you to help me."

"You could be lying!"

"I swear I'm telling you the truth!"

"If you're not lying, tell me who Garth is. You dealt with him and the girl!"

"I dealt only with Lorna," he said. "Garth never showed himself."

"I don't believe it," she whispered back tensely.

"He was clever. Some crook from the continent. All she ever told me about him was that he wore an eye patch."

"You could wear one. Anyone could."

"I am not Garth!"

"Why did you register in the hotel under that name?"

"I was trying to make a final deal to buy them off. You were getting increasingly upset about her visits to the house. I decided it would be easier at a hotel. She suggested that I register under Garth's name so we could make easy contact."

Ishbel listened to his version of the mixed-up affair and saw that it might have happened that way. Still she was wary of accepting his word for it. It could too easily be a clever lie.

She said, "I can't trust you! I can't trust anyone!"

"I am your husband!"

"That makes no difference if you're a murderer," she told him.

"Help me get out of here and I'll prove I'm not."

"I have only your word for that."

"I will," he said. "At least let me stay here for a little."

She said, "I should shoot you and then cry for help. Dr. Gregory is just across the hall."

"Don't do that!" he pleaded.

"I need to think about it," she said, reluctant to shoot him and yet not wanting to cooperate with him. "Go back in the closet."

He hesitated. "Don't betray me!"

"Back inside the closet," she said, raising the pistol.

He did as he was told. The door of the closet was shut. But now she knew he was in there. What to do? She had given her promise she would alert the others if she discovered anyone. But if she called them, Henry would be turned over to the police and likely tagged as the killer, Garth. Perhaps he was Garth! And if she helped him, he might turn on her at any minute and snuff out her life!

Did she have any real choice?

She was never to know what her decision might have been, for at that moment the door from the corridor was suddenly thrown open and she saw a figure standing on the threshold with a knife upraised. She had a glimpse of a face with a black eye patch. Then the draft from the door blew the candle out, and she was left in the darkness with the horror advancing on her!

She screamed and fired blindly into the darkness. The bullet did not hit her stalker, but the flash of fire from the pistol showed him close by her bed with the knife high in the air, ready to plunge into her!

She screamed again and felt the knife graze her arm as it came swooping down to bury itself in the mattress. She tried to escape but found herself pinned on the bed by strong, viciously cruel hands!

Then she was aware that the attacker was turning from her to battle with a third party. She knew that Henry had come to her rescue! She crawled across the bed to the other side of the room and then backed up to the wall as the battle between the two men went on.

Suddenly Detective Hawker appeared in the doorway of the bedroom with a lantern held high in his hand. He shouted out an order, and several of his bobbies came into the room to join the melee. When it was over, they had the man with the black patch securely held.

The stout detective lifted the lantern close to the face of the gasping murderer and with a swift movement snatched the black patch from his eye. It was only then that Ishbel recognized the features of Peter Graves!

"Take him away!" Detective Hawker said gruffly. And the bobbies dragged out the still struggling and infuriated artist.

Ishbel weakly crossed to her husband. "Did he hurt you?"

Henry was still breathless from his struggle. He shook his head. "He'd lost the knife by the time he got to me. I can't believe it was Graves."

Detective Hawker said, "I've had my eye on him from the start. He spent a lot of his time on the Continent. He had been Patricia's lover, and when he saw Lorna, he recognized at once that she must be related to his former mistress. From then on in he played two roles, himself and Reginald Garth. His blackmail scheme worked well enough for a time, but they became careless as the drugs took a tighter hold on them."

Henry said, "I hope you're satisfied about me now."

"You'll still have to satisfy the court that you were a victim of the blackmail and not part of it," the stout man warned him.

"Lord Carney will testify to that," Henry said.

The detective told him, "You can be grateful that you had a wife who never gave up her faith in you even at the darkest moment."

"I'm well aware of that," Henry said, placing an arm around her.

Ishbel had a sudden, unhappy thought. "Dr. Gregory! What can have happened to him?"

"The old man!" Detective Hawker said, turning.

Mrs. Needles was in the doorway to answer their question. "That villain has killed him! He's stretched out on the floor of his bedroom!"

They all rushed across the hall. Detective Hawker bent down by the old man. After a moment, he said, "He's not dead. He's had a bash on his head to silence him. But if I know his sort, he'll survive that!"

As it turned out Detective Hawker was right. But then, Ishbel decided, he generally was. Peter Graves was scheduled to be tried for murder. He refused to see or talk to anyone, and his physical condition deteriorated following his arrest. His long addiction to drugs had left him with a wrecked constitution. In the grim atmosphere of a prison cell his health worsened rapidly.

Henry was so sickened by the scandalous affair that he did what Ishbel had pleaded with him to do for several years: he sold the family business and washed his hands of any further traffic in drugs.

He made the announcement at a dinner party at Number Twenty-Two a few weeks after the capture and arrest of Peter Graves. Mrs. Needles outdid herself for the occasion, since there were a number of special guests. Scots food was served for the occasion, since a number of those present were from North of the Border.

Henry sat at one end of the table and carved the roast of

lamb. Haggis was served and was greeted with loud murmurs of approval. Ishbel sat at the other end of the long table with her Uncle Walter on her left and Dr. Jock Gregory on her right. The little man still had a bandaged head, but he was well on his way to normal health again.

Cousin Ernest was there, along with special guests Lawyer Timothy Slade and Detective Hawker. The stout man smiled at them all and said, "I have no doubt that this is the last time I'll see any of you."

Cousin Ernest laughed. "I should hope so. None of us want to find ourselves in trouble with the police!"

"I offer a toast to New Scotland Yard and the man who made it all a reality, Sir Robert Peel," Henry said, rising with his wine glass in hand.

They all drank the toast. Detective Hawker said, "I thank you. You made an unpleasant duty as easy as possible. While I regret the violence, I am thankful the crimes were solved and the villain behind them all was brought to justice."

Lawyer Timothy Slade said, "Lord Carney asked me to express his thanks to you all. And particularly to you, Detective Hawker, for keeping the unpleasant affair as quiet as possible."

"Nobody would gain by a scandal," the stout detective said.

It was then that Henry rose and made his announcement of his sale of the business. He ended with, "I have decided to buy a cattle farm in Scotland and become a farmer!"

Ishbel's smile from the end of the table would have been reward enough without her warmly said, "Dearest Henry!"

He came down the length of the table and kissed her, to loud applause and laughter. Then he said, "I knew I had to reinstate her with her family or lose her!"

"Hear! Hear!" said stern Uncle Walter, looking quite

unlike his usually grim self.

Dr. Jock Gregory raised his hand for silence. "Since this has become an occasion for reunion, I have something to say!"

"By all means, Dr. Gregory!" Ishbel urged him.

The old doctor chuckled. "I bounced her on my knee when she was a little baby! Now I have to ask the sophisticated lady for permission to have my say!"

"No orations," Uncle Walter told his friend. "Get on with whatever it is you have in your crop!"

Dr. Jock Gregory rose and bowed to them all. "I have had too much wine. I am a little drunk."

"We know that," Ernest teased him. "Now tell us the rest!"

"Wretched youth," the old doctor said with a twinkle in his eyes. "Let me tell you all I have made a discovery."

"What sort of discovery?" Ishbel asked.

Dr. Gregory glanced in the direction of Detective Hawker and said, "I had a suspicion, and I turned to this good man to help me."

"A small thing, Doctor," the detective said modestly.

"Not really," Dr. Gregory replied. "When I first came here I was impressed by the gardener, Simpson."

Henry said, "The poor fellow was under suspicion for a time because of his black eye patch."

"Which came honorably enough from his service in the navy under Nelson," Ishbel said.

"You hired him, didn't you?" Dr. Gregory asked.

"Yes," she said.

"What was your reason?"

She said, "He seemed a nice old man and I thought I would like him for a gardener."

Dr. Gregory said, "You felt you would like to have him

around. He appealed to you as a person."

Walter Stewart groaned. "Enough of this beating around the bush, Gregory. Let us hear whatever it is you are trying to say."

The little doctor bowed. "I'm coming to it. Detective Hawker had information about Simpson. He knew he was an ex-convict and that he had served time for a crime of violence. Years ago, when he was tried, there was a great deal of uncertainty about whether he was the guilty party, but they managed to convict him. He felt the disgrace deeply, and when he emerged from prison he changed his name."

Ishbel said, "His name is not Simpson?"

"No," the little doctor said triumphantly, "it is not Simpson." He turned to Detective Hawker and asked him, "Tell him the name under which he was convicted."

Detective Hawker said, "His name was Stewart, William Stewart!"

There was a long moment of silent amazement at the table. Then Walter Stewart jumped up and in an excited voice exclaimed, "Are you telling us that Simpson is Billy Stewart, the lad who was long ago lost in battle?"

"That is what I'm saying and what I believe to be true," Dr. Jock Gregory said. "I saw him often when he was a youth. He still retains some of the same features I knew then, despite his age and the battering life has given him."

Walter Stewart said, "But Billy died! That was the word we had!"

"He sent that word back because it was what he wanted," the doctor said. "He wanted to live his own life away from the family. It suited him to be dead."

Ishbel said, "And later, when he found himself in trouble with the law, he felt he never could rejoin the family. So he changed his name."

"He did," the old doctor said. "And by a freak you decided

to hire him. They say blood calls to blood, and I believe this to be true in the case of you and Billy."

Ernest said, "But I've always thought of Billy as a lad. He died as a young man. This Simpson is old!"

Thin Dr. Gregory said, "We all grow old in time, my boy. You will find that out. Billy was born in 1770, so it is perfectly natural that he be sixty-one now. Don't forget I'm eighty-four, and if your grandfather Ian—bless his memory—were alive, he'd be eighty-six!"

Walter Stewart's stern face was a study in astonishment. He said, "I don't know whether to believe you or not."

Henry said, "There's an easy way to settle it. We'll have him come in."

He called to Chen and asked the old Chinese to go out to the garden where Simpson often sat in the evening and get him. Simpson had returned the morning after the murder with no explanation for his absence except that he'd been frightened of the police.

Ishbel had lost her fear of Chen when she'd learned from her husband that he had instructed Chen to watch over her, and that Chen on his own initiative had placed the pistol in her dresser for her use.

There were murmurings of astonishment around the table as they waited for Chen to return with the gardener. At last Simpson came into the room looking embarrassed, his cap held in his hands.

The small Dr. Gregory went over to the big man and placed a hand on his arm. "It is all right, Simpson," he said. "I have told them."

The big man with the eye patch looked at Ishbel earnestly and said, "I trust you will not dismiss me because of it, ma'am."

"Dismiss you!" Ishbel said incredulously. "I should say

not! You will come to Scotland with us, along with Mrs. Nee-dles and Chen. But you will be our foreman, not our gar-dener. You deserve better! You are one of the family!"

"I was like my father," Billy said contritely. "I brought shame to the Stewarts. I do not deserve to be considered one of you!"

"Ridiculous!" It was Walter Stewart who spoke up and went to the big man. "You have our blood! Great Aunt Peggy was your mother. You will take your rightful place among us. And I say that as the head of the family!"

Ishbel warned Simpson, "Better agree with him, Uncle Billy. He has a way of dealing with those Stewarts who don't."

A broad smile crossed the old man's face. "Uncle Billy!" he repeated after her. "I like the sound of that!"

So what had begun in mystery, fear, and violence ended in a warm family reunion. Simpson spent much of the evening seated in the living room discussing events of the old days at Stormhaven with Walter Stewart and little Dr. Gregory. By the time the evening was over, it was clear that he was be-having more like a Stewart and less like Simpson.

After the guests departed, Ishbel and Henry found them-selves alone and blessedly content for the first time in a long while.

She asked him, "Will you miss London and the tea busi-ness?"

"No more than you missed Edinburgh and your family," he said. "I look forward to getting to know the Stewarts of Stormhaven better!"

He took her in his arms. She gazed up at him with a gentle smile and said softly, "Just as long as you remain in love with one of us!"

"That will always be," he promised her as he touched his lips to hers.